"I think I need to apologize."

"Sure. But there are no apologies necessary."

"No?" Gabe eyed her uncertainly. "Look, that was… I'm not hitting on you."

"Great." She wasn't sure if that was an improvement.

"That doesn't clear it up. I mean, yes, I find you attractive. More than attractive—gorgeous. I always have. That's no excuse."

"But it wasn't only you."

"It wasn't?" He raised his eyebrows. "You sure about that?"

"I felt it, too. But obviously, we can't go there."

"Obviously. You're my daughter's mother. And you and I have to maintain a good relationship for her sake. We can't just try this on for size and change our minds later without it affecting Zoey."

"We're blessed, in a way. We don't have some failed romance between us. We're better for it."

"And we need to keep it that way. I know that, and I won't…let things get complicated. If that makes you feel any better."

So they were on the same page. But it didn't exactly fix whatever attraction was stewing between them.

Patricia Johns writes from Alberta, Canada. She has her Hon. BA in English literature and currently writes for Harlequin's Love Inspired, Western Romance and Heartwarming lines. You can find her at patriciajohnsromance.com.

Books by Patricia Johns

Love Inspired

Comfort Creek Lawmen

Deputy Daddy
The Lawman's Runaway Bride
The Deputy's Unexpected Family

His Unexpected Family
The Rancher's City Girl
A Firefighter's Promise
The Lawman's Surprise Family

Harlequin Heartwarming

A Baxter's Redemption
The Runaway Bride
A Boy's Christmas Wish

Visit the Author Profile page at Harlequin.com for more titles.

The Deputy's
Unexpected Family

Patricia Johns

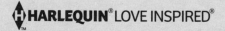
HARLEQUIN® LOVE INSPIRED®

Recycling programs
for this product may
not exist in your area.

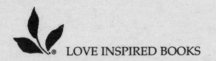

® LOVE INSPIRED BOOKS

ISBN-13: 978-1-335-50968-0

The Deputy's Unexpected Family

Copyright © 2018 by Patricia Johns

www.Harlequin.com

Printed in U.S.A.

Every good gift and every perfect gift is from above, and cometh down from the Father of lights, with whom is no variableness, neither shadow of turning.
—*James* 1:17

To my husband,
my very own Happily Ever After. And to
our son, who is old enough now that he really
hates being left out of book dedications!

Chapter One

Harper Kemp stood in the center of her disheveled shop, Blessings Bridal, gaping at the mess. She had arrived two hours before any of the other shops on Sycamore Avenue opened for the day, hoping to get a little paperwork done, but had walked into this.

The front display window was edged in the sharp lace of broken glass and a chill autumn wind whisked into the shop. The cash register hung open, empty, and several voluminous gowns clung to the mannequins in tatters. Whoever had done this had slashed through the delicate material, leaving the floor littered with beads. The front display case had been smashed, and the velvet nests that once held tiaras, clasps, bejeweled belts and the like now lay vacant, peppered with glittering glass.

Her heart slammed in her chest, and she pulled her ginger curls away from her face as she took it all in. Why hadn't the alarm gone off when this happened?

Comfort Creek was a small town with an inordinate number of cops roaming the streets due to a county-run sensitivity training course based in the town. It was supposed to be the safest community in Colorado due to their overabundance of officers patrolling the town while they completed their sensitivity training. Tell that to whomever had robbed her.

"Oh, Lord…" It was a prayer, but she was still too stunned to know what to even ask for. She pulled her tortoiseshell glasses off her face and glanced down at her phone. She'd just called the police and given the pertinent information. They'd be here soon, she was assured. She ran a hand through her fiery curls. A few months ago, Harper got custody of her four-year-old goddaughter, Zoey, when her best friend, Andrea, died in a car accident, and she felt like she'd just found her footing again with a daughter to raise…now this.

Harper stepped over the broken glass, already mentally tallying up the loss. Insurance would cover most of it…except Heidi's dress! The thought struck and her stomach dropped. Her younger sister's wedding dress was a family heirloom, and no amount of insurance money would cover the sentimental value of that dress.

Harper dashed into the back room and spotted the untouched box high on a shelf. She breathed a prayer of thanks. God must have put His hand over that dress… and she was grateful. Everything else could be replaced. How was that for some perspective?

The bell from the front door jingled, and she heard the tramping of heavy feet.

"Miss Kemp?" a deep male voice reverberated through the store, and Harper turned back toward the retail space. The police had arrived.

"I'm here," she said, stepping back out. "Thanks for—"

The words evaporated on her tongue. The officer standing in the middle of the mess was tall, muscled and had the same direct gray gaze she remembered from years ago when they were teenagers dreaming of their futures in this town… It was Gabe Banks.

"Hey—" His tone softened. "Long time."

"Very long time," she agreed, then smiled feebly. "What are you doing here?"

"You reported a robbery." He raised one eyebrow.

"I mean in Comfort Creek. I thought you were in Fort Collins." One possibility bloomed in her mind—that he had somehow found out about four-year-old Zoey. There were enough people in this town who would have pieced it together…

Gabe's expression grew more guarded, then he shrugged. "Sensitivity training. What else? Comfort Creek has me for two weeks."

"Oh." That was reasonable. Comfort Creek saw a constant influx of officers doing sensitivity training. What had Gabe done to garner this honor?

"So…" Gabe pulled out a pad of paper. "What happened here?"

"I have no idea," she said. "I just arrived, found it like this and called 911."

"Any idea how much was taken?" he asked.

"Not yet. I'm still kind of in shock."

He took a few notes, poked his head back outside the door and appeared to be doing his job for a few minutes while Harper stood where he'd left her, feeling in the way in her own shop.

"I heard about Andrea's passing," he said as he came back inside. "I'm sorry. She was…special. And I know how close you two were."

Special. That's how Gabe referred to a woman he'd dated for a year? Maybe he didn't feel like he had a right to sympathy for the passing of his ex-girlfriend he hadn't seen or spoken to in the last five years. And maybe he was right about that.

"We really were," she said. "I miss her. So does Zoey."

"That's her daughter?" Gabe clarified.

Harper nodded. "Zoey's four. I'm her guardian now."

Gabe shot her a sympathetic smile, then glanced away. Andrea had never told Gabe the truth about Zoey.

"Did anyone tell you about the father?" she asked cautiously.

"My grandmother said that she was on the rebound after me," he replied. "Grandma was a little more judgmental than that, but that was the gist of it."

A flat-out lie, but it was the story Andrea had put around.

"Well, Zoey is a sweetheart," Harper said. "We're doing all right, but it's hard with Andrea gone."

"Yeah, I can imagine." A couple of beats passed between them—an awkward pause.

"Anyway," Harper said, clearing her throat. "Back to the robbery."

"When did you find this?" he asked, professional reserve back in place.

"This morning when I came in. Ten minutes ago," she replied. "With all the patrol on these streets, I'm surprised no one noticed it earlier." She paused, a thought suddenly occurring to her. Gabe was here on disciplinary action—how much authority did he really have? She was tired, had a lot to deal with today, obviously, and didn't have time to waste.

"Are you supposed to be taking cases?" she asked

with a slight frown. "I mean, will I have to repeat this all over again with another officer?"

Gabe shot her a flat look. "Yes, I can take cases. Dispatch assigned me. You want to take that up with the chief? Get a less ornery officer, or something? I'm not here because I'm bad at my job. I'm here for being mouthy with my boss."

She smiled wanly. "I was just checking."

"So, we're okay here, then?" he said, tucking a thumb in his belt. "Because if you'd rather have some other cop take over, I'm sure I can go patrol the school zones or something."

She heard the sarcasm in that gravelly tone, and she felt heat in her cheeks. He'd always been like this—brash, opinionated and stubborn as all get-out.

"I'm sure you'll be fine," she said. It might be time to let some old resentments go. "It's been a rough day so far, so maybe cut me some slack."

He eyed her for a moment, then scanned the scene. "We'll take fingerprints. I'm not expecting to get too much, though. I noticed both the phone and alarm lines were cut outside."

"That would explain why my alarm didn't go off."

"This was no smash and grab," Gabe confirmed. "This was planned."

"In the best-patrolled town in Colorado," she said.

Gabe didn't answer. His boots crunched over broken glass as he headed toward the display case. "We'll need a complete list of anything missing. Descriptions would be good, pictures if you have them. We'll be watching pawn shops and online sale sites. Whatever they took, they'll be selling."

Harper felt her eyes mist. The immensity of the damage and the work ahead of her to clean up was just starting to sink in. She'd have to call her dad—the owner of the store—and tell him what happened, too…

"How much cash was in the register?" Gabe asked.

"Just change—I made the deposit last night," she replied. "There was about a hundred and sixty dollars in the drawer."

"Approximately how much was the merchandise worth in the case?" he asked.

"Five or six thousand. Those were all Swarovski crystals."

"Was there anything under this case?" Gabe asked from across the room, and Harper looked up with a start. The veil—her grandmother's wedding veil that Heidi was going to use for her wedding…that Harper hoped to wear one day for her own wedding…

"Yes," she said. "A pink box…shoe box size. It's not there?"

She crossed the room to where Gabe squatted next to the display case. The space beneath it was empty, and a lump rose in her throat.

"What was in the box?" he asked.

"My grandmother's veil," she said woodenly. "It's not replaceable."

Harper wiped a tear that escaped her lid and pushed herself back to her feet. She had no intention of crying in front of Gabe Banks. This was all a pretty big shock, and adding a missing family heirloom to the mix was more than she could handle with grace and dignity at the moment.

Gabe rose to his feet, too, and she was struck by the sheer size of him. He'd always been tall, but the past decade had solidified him into steely manhood. This was no longer the lanky, cocky teenager.

"Hey." His tone softened. "I don't have a lot to do around here for the next two weeks. I'll pour all my bad attitude into your case."

She blinked back her tears. "Would you do that?"

"What else am I supposed to do with my time? I think that's the idea—give us some peace and quiet to sort out our personal issues."

"And you want some distraction from that?" she asked with a small smile.

"What can I say—I'm comfortable with my skeletons. That's why you never liked me much."

"I liked you fine," she said with a shake of her head. He raised one eyebrow, and she felt the heat come back to her face. "I just didn't think you were good for Andrea," she conceded.

She hadn't been blind to his charm and good looks back then—she'd just known better than to let herself fall for him, too. All the girls swooned over Gabe Banks. He'd been filled with flirtation and laughter in some moments, and then brooding and distanced in others. What teenage girl could resist such a "complicated" guy? Harper, that's who.

"Well, you were right about that," he said. "I wasn't any good for her. So, no hard feelings."

At least he recognized that much. Still, she found herself searching his features for Zoey—his eyes, the shape of his ears. Zoey looked a lot like Andrea, but she wasn't an exact replica of her mother, either. She had dark hair like her dad, and the tiny cleft in her chin was Gabe's, too. This was Zoey's father, and she'd have to figure out her next move in that department. So far, she'd been focused on finding her balance as Zoey's new mother, but she'd never been entirely comfortable with Andrea's decision to keep Zoey a secret. Zoey would be asking about her father eventually, but Harper was now faced with a dilemma of her own: Should she tell Gabe about his daughter, or should she let it lie?

Gabe walked around Blessings Bridal collecting evidence and taking notes for the next hour. He'd never been inside this shop in all the years he lived in Comfort Creek, but he'd passed it often enough. Everyone knew the Kemps, and Blessings Bridal serviced all the brides in the surrounding small towns.

Eight other cops arrived to help—far more than needed, obviously, but there wasn't anything else happening around Comfort Creek, and the temptation to lend a hand was too great for both the other officers and the locals. It took two officers at the outside door to keep curious locals moving along.

From where Gabe stood brushing for prints, he glanced over at Harper. She lingered in the doorway to the back room. Her red curls hung around her shoulders, and her gaze moved from officer to officer, watching them work. Her glasses were off again, and she had the end in her mouth. She was gorgeous, and Gabe pulled his gaze away from her, pushing back the thought.

"Gabe." Officer Bryce Camden approached, and he rose to his feet, dropping the brush back into a protective plastic bag. He and Bryce knew each other from their days on the Fort Collins force. Gabe met Bryce beside a rack of wedding dresses that appeared to be untouched.

"Any of this look familiar?" Bryce asked.

Gabe glanced around. "It's definitely not a smash and grab. The phone and security system lines were cut outside. Besides a few display dresses being trashed, these ones are untouched. They knew what they were aiming for. I'm guessing professionals."

"I had three cases back in Fort Collins that match this MO," Bryce said. "The cut lines, the small amount of trashing, as if for appearances, and a select amount of highly salable merchandise taken."

"Anyone caught?" Gabe asked.

Bryce shook his head. "Still at large. But there were other sites hit across Fort Collins—always spread out, and a couple of months between each. They were careful."

"Yeah, I remember that," Gabe agreed, the details coming back to him. "I had one of those cases—a jewelry store."

"They may be spreading to smaller communities where people aren't quite as security conscious," Bryce suggested.

It was a definite possibility, and Gabe's mind clicked through what he could remember of those cases. None had been solved, and the first hit on every store hadn't been too bad. In and out. Quick. A few things taken. The perps were scoping things out more than anything.

"They always came back for a second hit on every location," Gabe said. "Within days or weeks. And that's when they cleaned the place out. There was an old man who was shot, trying to defend his store that second time around."

"I remember that." Bryce nodded. "So if we're looking at the same people, they'll be back. I'm sure the chief will agree that we'll need to keep a pretty close eye on the place for the next couple of weeks."

Gabe signed the bottom of a form he was filling out as first on the scene, and glanced over toward Harper.

"I knew her—as kids. Teenagers. I dated her best friend," Gabe said.

"Yeah?" Bryce nodded. "That might be useful. Why not offer to help out in the cleanup? Just...be here for a bit."

Back in the day, Gabe would have jumped at the chance. He'd had a thing for Harper Kemp, but she'd been steps above him. She was smart, cute, had a plan for her future... And he'd been a messed-up teenager whose grandmother ran him down on a nightly basis. He'd asked her out once, and she'd turned him down flat. He hadn't tried again.

Looking at Harper now with those sad green eyes and her arms crossed protectively over her chest, all those old feelings from years ago came flooding back. Harper never acted like she needed him—or any guy—but she still sparked that protective instinct inside of him. He wanted to offer something, and with this uniform—at least for the next two weeks—he could.

"I could go plainclothes and keep an eye out," Gabe said. "We want to catch these guys, not just scare them off."

"My thoughts exactly," Bryce confirmed. "If we can be ready for their next hit, we might be able to take these guys in. Let me check in with the chief, and I'll confirm if we've got a plan."

Bryce pulled out his cell phone and walked a few feet away to make his call. Gabe shoved the form into his back pocket. He was here to do his time and then head back to Fort Collins. Period. It was humiliating enough to be back under these circumstances. However, catching a robbery gang might make his stay here less agonizing. He'd go back to Fort Collins as a success, instead of chastised.

"What's going on?" Harper asked, coming up beside Gabe.

"We're thinking that this looks similar to a few cases in Fort Collins," Gabe replied.

"That's good, right?" Harper brightened.

"Well…" He shrugged. "Not really. They have an MO of returning to the scene and hitting it again a little while later, after they've scoped the place out and have a better idea of what they're aiming at."

Harper paled. "I *have* a security system. It didn't do much good."

"Like I said, they're pros," Gabe said, and when he saw the nervousness flicker across her features, he realized that she needed reassurance, not more reason to be afraid.

"So what should I do?" Harper asked.

At that moment, Bryce headed across the store in their direction and gave Gabe a decisive nod. When he reached them, he said, "It's a go."

"What's a 'go'?" Harper asked, her attention swinging between them.

"We need a police presence around here for a little while to protect you, but it can't be too obvious, ma'am," Bryce replied. "Officer Banks will be here today, and he'll keep an eye out for your safety and for any…unusual activity in the area."

Harper froze for a moment, then shot Gabe a quizzical look, one eyebrow raised.

"It's for your safety," Gabe said with a small smile. "Besides, this is now about the chief's orders."

She'd probably prefer a different officer, maybe even Bryce—safely married and constantly gushing about his toddler daughter. Gabe had already heard more about that baby than he knew about any other kid at the moment, and he'd only been back in town for a day.

"We thought that since you know each other already, it might make things less awkward. Officer Banks has offered to help clean the place up once the paperwork is done." Bryce's lips turned up in a small, ironic smile.

"You did?" Harper's expression softened.

"Yeah."

"That's really kind." Harper sighed. "It would definitely help. Dad's health hasn't been great lately, and I've been dreading telling him about this. But if I can tell him that we've got a plainclothes officer at the store—"

"We're just about done gathering evidence," Bryce broke in. "So we'll be out of your hair in a few minutes. Officer Banks can take it from there."

Bryce headed toward the front door, and Gabe glanced down at Harper. She was rigid, her spine ramrod straight and her lips pressed together in a thin line. Harper looked slowly up at him. "How much danger are we in, Gabe? Be honest."

Her green eyes locked on to him, and he felt a surge of longing. It had been more than ten years since he'd had an unrequited crush on this woman, and one look from her still made him wish he could be some sort of superhero for her.

"Significantly less if I'm around." He shot her a grin. "I'm trained to deal with this stuff. Trust me on that."

Harper sighed. Did she recognize the difference between a messed-up teen and a fully trained police officer? He was particularly adept in hand-to-hand combat, and he was the best shot in Fort Collins. She was safe in his hands, and he was no longer that kid she couldn't take seriously. He was every inch a man now.

"Let me keep an eye on the place, and you can focus on the stuff you need to take care of," Gabe said, adding, "like Andrea's little girl."

She nodded, then said softly, "Her name is Zoey."

"Zoey," he repeated. It seemed to matter to her that he recognize Andrea's daughter a little more directly. But he'd never been very good with kids, and it wasn't going to start now. She could take care of her business, and he'd take care of her. Intimidating bad guys and protecting the vulnerable—that part he was good at. Kids and family were his weaknesses, and yet he was back in Fort Collins where he had his own family history to face.

He could endure anything for two weeks.

Chapter Two

The next morning, Harper unlocked the front door for Blessings Bridal and let Zoey go in first. She paused and looked along the street. It was the same familiar road—sun dappled with intermittent trees spreading long branches over the asphalt. All was quiet, as it normally was this time of day, the only sound that of a chattering squirrel. A police cruiser eased slowly down the street. The officer—a woman—gave her a quick wave.

Harper had slept terribly the night before. Her father was worried now—which was to be expected even after she'd assured him that she had it all under control. And now Harper was faced with the paperwork from the insurance company.

"Let me help you, sweetheart," her father had said. "I'm retired, not dead!"

But Harper didn't want his help; she *needed* to take care of the robbery paperwork on her own. If she was going to be opening a second store in Comfort Creek— a maternity shop—she'd better prove to more than just herself that she could handle the stress and the demands. There had been more than one well-meaning person who had questioned if she could raise a young child while running *this* shop… So while it was all well and good to say she had nothing to prove to anyone, she did.

Running Blessings Bridal was satisfying in its own right, but she wanted more—a store with her own name on the bottom line, not her father's. Besides, this store was all that her father had to will to Harper and Heidi, and since it would be the bulk of their inheritance, that was going to be complicated. Eventually, at least. The second shop, Blessings Maternity, was going to be Harper's first personal foray into the business world, and she wanted it so badly that she could taste it.

"It's all messed up!" Zoey said, looking around the store. Harper pulled the door shut and locked it after them. She and Gabe had boarded over the broken window yesterday, and the glass and mess was mostly cleaned up. The display case still sat vacant.

"I know, sweetie. Someone broke in. I told you about that, right? So now we have to clean it up." Harper put the boxed wedding dress on the counter. She'd brought it home with her last night—not taking any chances on a family heirloom—but the sewing machine and all the tools she'd need for the fitting were here in the shop.

Zoey went to the display case and sighed. "The crowns are gone."

Zoey loved the tiaras, and when the shop was closed, Harper would let her try them on in front of the full-length mirror. It had started when Andrea would visit after hours, and Zoey would sit on her mother's lap and stare at her reflection with a crystal tiara on her little head.

"I know. The insurance company will give us money so we can get more. You can help me choose them."

"Today?" Zoey asked hopefully.

"Not today. We're going to do a fitting for Aunt Heidi's wedding dress," Harper said. "And you get to help."

Since the store was temporarily closed, Harper had pulled Zoey out of preschool for a few days. Preschool had been a constant for Zoey from before her mother passed away, but a few days of girl time would be good for them, too, Harper decided. Besides, it was broad daylight, and she highly doubted that anyone would come back to rob the place at this time of day.

"It's our wedding dress, right?" Zoey was still working out how all of this worked.

"Yes, it's our dress. My grandmother wore that dress when she got married a very long time ago. And now Aunt Heidi is going to wear it for her wedding. And maybe you'll even wear it for yours."

If there was enough of it left. If Heidi didn't demand so many alterations that there was nothing salvageable for another bride...

"Grandma Jane..." Zoey said softly.

"No, Great-Grandma Kemp." Harper sighed. Six months wasn't really long enough for Zoey to embrace all the extra family, let alone fully understand what ancestors were. She was four. She knew about the family she saw on a regular basis, which included Andrea's mom, Grandma Jane, and Harper's mom, Grandma Georgia. Having two grandmas was as much as Zoey seemed able to wrap her mind around right now. And having a new mother...

Harper opened the box on the counter and looked down at the familiar material. It was a gown from 1950—A-line taffeta covered in lace with sheer lace sleeves and décolletage. The dress had fit their grandmother at ankle length, but Grandma Kemp had been a petite woman, and Heidi was significantly taller, so Harper was guessing it would fit her sister at a tea length—perfect for today's fashion.

There was a tap at the front door, and Harper looked up to see Heidi through the unbroken window. She wore a leather jacket and a pair of jeans, a floppy leather bag tossed over one shoulder. A pair of sunglasses was perched on top of her short-cropped auburn hair.

"Auntie Heidi!" Zoey announced, and Harper crossed the store and unlocked the door. As Heidi came inside, she glanced around. She'd dropped by yesterday and seen the state of things—as had a quarter of the town— so it wasn't a shock.

"So where's Gabe?" Heidi asked.

"I don't know. He's not going to be here every second," Harper replied. "The police are doing a lot of drive-bys, though."

"Hmm." Heidi ruffled Zoey's hair. "And how's my favorite flower girl?"

"I'm good!" Zoey sang out. She was excited to be in Heidi's wedding, and Harper was grateful to her sister for including her new daughter. Anything that made Zoey feel more accepted and at home was a plus.

While Heidi deposited her bag and sunglasses on a nearby chair, Harper pulled the antique dress out of the box. It had been stored impeccably over the years, and while the lace had darkened over time, it was still a stunning dress by any standard.

"Is he still as good-looking as he used to be?" Heidi asked.

"Good looks only go so far," Harper replied. But yes, he was—more so. He'd matured into a ruggedly handsome man with a steely gaze that could make a woman's stomach flip. But what use was that when a man's character didn't match up?

"Does he…know?" Heidi murmured as Zoey took the sunglasses to the mirror to try them on.

"No." Harper knew what her sister was asking, and she didn't want to say too much within Zoey's hearing distance. "He seems completely oblivious."

"Are you going to tell him?" Heidi glanced toward Zoey, too, but the girl seemed rapt in her game of dress up.

"I don't know," Harper admitted quietly. "I feel like I should. He deserves to know at least, doesn't he?"

"Andrea didn't think so." Heidi met Harper's gaze and held it.

"That was a personal grudge, though," Harper said. Andrea had been deeply hurt by Gabe's inability to commit to her, and she'd never been able to forgive him. She said he hadn't wanted to be a husband or a father, and she was protecting her daughter from the ultimate rejection. But Zoey was his daughter, and meeting her in person might change that.

"Something can be both personal and the right choice," Heidi replied softly.

"One day, Zoey's going to ask about her dad, and what then?" Harper asked. She couldn't lie to her daughter, and without a really good reason otherwise, Harper couldn't lie to Gabe, either. "I'd hoped to be able to put off thinking about Gabe until another time. But with him in town, I'm going to have to face this sooner than I thought."

Zoey tired of her game and came back to where they were standing. She wore the sunglasses perched on the top of her little head the way she'd seen Heidi wear them, and they slipped and dropped to the floor. Heidi bent to pick them up.

Harper gently shook the dress out of its folds and held it aloft for her sister to see in full length. Heidi slowly rose from her crouch to collect the glasses, her gaze moving over the dress in wonder.

"This is it..." Heidi breathed.

"Grandma's dress."

No one had worn the dress since Grandma Kemp, and while Harper had done a few repairs where the lining had fallen apart, nothing else was changed.

"I'm thinking it will fit you at about a tea length." Harper went on. "We'll have to let out the waist a little bit...since I'm pretty sure you don't want to be squeezing yourself into a 1950s girdle. And Grandma was tiny."

Heidi chuckled. "No girdle. And I want to shorten it to above the knee."

"Above the knee?" Harper gathered the dress back up and put it on top of the box. "That's not even funny."

"I'm not joking," Heidi retorted. "I don't see myself as a traditional bride anyway."

"Not traditional?" Harper retorted. "Heidi, you quit your job to marry this man! If that isn't traditional, I don't know what is!"

"Planning a society wedding is going to be a full-time job in itself," Heidi said. "Besides, I obviously won't need the income anymore. It's not like the job was my dream career. I was a receptionist."

"That job was *yours*," Harper countered. "That matters. Keeping something that belongs to you..." Harper sighed. In her humble opinion, her sister was fighting the wrong battle over keeping some independence. Heidi was waging war for a dress, but she'd given up her job. "I'm just saying, Chris's family is very traditional. You're marrying into one of the wealthiest families in the county. If you leave the dress as is, it'll be tea length. So midcalf."

"That's long, Harper."

Harper rolled her eyes. "Do you have to be so different all the time?"

"I'll still be me," Heidi quipped. "Difficult as always. Thankfully, Chris thinks I'm pretty."

"You'll want nice pictures. And so will he, for that matter."

"I'll want pictures that show me as me," Heidi countered. "I have never in my life worn a long dress anywhere. I'm a jeans girl. So I think a short, flirty dress is a nice compromise."

"And hack apart Grandma's dress?" Harper gaped at her sister.

"We could use the leftover material in a flower girl dress for Zoey." Heidi shrugged, a smile coming to her face. "It would be perfect!"

It would be perfect for Heidi, but what about any chance of Harper wearing her grandmother's dress for her own wedding one day? What about Zoey's wedding?

"I want to wear it, too," Harper confessed.

"We always said that the first sister to get married would wear it," Heidi interjected.

"We were teenagers at the time," Harper replied. "And quite frankly, being the older sister, I'd assumed that would fall to me."

"Well, sorry to beat you to it!" Tears sparkled in

Heidi's eyes. "So what are you saying—you won't alter the dress for me?"

Harper didn't answer. She wasn't sure what she was saying.

"Why don't you use the veil," Heidi said. "I never wanted a veil anyway. I want a little fascinator like people do in London weddings."

"The veil is gone," Harper said woodenly. "It was taken in the robbery."

She met her sister's gaze and they were both silent for a moment. Heidi sighed.

"I didn't know…"

"It would have been fair, though," Harper said after a moment. "I might have agreed to that."

Tears misted Harper's gaze and she looked down at Zoey, who was staring up at them, her gray eyes wide.

"It's okay, Zoey," Harper said. "Auntie and I are just like little girls sometimes, and bicker. It's nothing to worry about."

"No biting," Zoey whispered, and Harper and Heidi burst out laughing.

Harper scooped her daughter up into her arms and gave her a squeeze. "That's solid advice, Zoey."

They'd figure out something, and Harper sent up a silent and slightly selfish prayer that their solution would leave her a piece of her grandmother's legacy for her own wedding day…and that she might be as blessed as her sister in the romance department. Heidi's fiancé, Chris, was a great guy—smart, loyal, sweet…

But even if she didn't find her own Mr. Right anytime soon, Harper had her daughter, whom she loved with all her heart. She'd never worn maternity clothes or given birth, but she knew that she was every bit a mom. Some blessings came along unexpected paths.

Gabe drove past Blessings Bridal on his way to the police station that morning. Everything looked as quiet as he expected. Passing the shop was out of his way, considering that he was staying at Lily and Bryce Camden's bed and breakfast. The department wouldn't pay for the entire cost of the B and B, but they subsidized it, which helped. And it was a whole lot more comfortable than the dive of a hotel he was going to be staying at originally. The breakfast that his hostess had prepared for him—apricot oatmeal, yogurt and a bowl of fresh fruit—made his stay feel more like a vacation than the reprimand that it was supposed to be. But this morning's meeting with Chief Morgan should take care of that.

He parked in the lot next to the precinct and glanced at his watch. Gabe had been dreading this part—the discipline. It would come in the form of training, but everyone knew what this was. Granted, Gabe should have kept his mouth shut when his boss irritated him, but he didn't think he'd been altogether wrong, either. Unfortunately, when it came to the chain of command, being right wasn't everything.

Gabe remembered Chance Morgan from the local force when he'd been a troubled teen in Comfort Creek. Chief Morgan had been a sergeant back then, and Gabe hadn't known him personally, but he still cared what the man thought of him. Gabe headed through the front doors and nodded to the receptionist, Cheryl. She was on the phone, but put the receiver against her shoulder to shield the mouthpiece and pointed toward the bull pen.

"The chief says to go straight to his office. He's waiting for you," she said with a smile.

Easy enough for her to smile. She wasn't the one facing binders full of sensitivity training. He'd heard horror stories of those questionnaires and required reading... all about how to "constructively approach disagreements and negotiate a win-win solution." Yeah, he'd had a buddy who did some sensitivity training in Fort Collins—apparently, not quite as in-depth as he was about to experience out here in Comfort Creek. If they had to physically send him away for the experience, he could only imagine what was in store.

He gave the receptionist a nod of thanks and headed around the bull pen toward the chief's office. He could dread it all he wanted. There was no way out of Comfort Creek but through the program.

"Come in," Chief Morgan called when Gabe knocked, and he opened the door.

Chief Morgan sat behind a desk. He looked to be about forty with sandy-blond hair that was just starting to gray. He appeared to be finishing some paperwork, and when Gabe came in, he flipped shut the folder and gave him a cordial nod.

"Have a seat, officer."

"Thank you, sir." Gabe shut the door behind him and eased into a chair.

"So, why are you here?"

Gabe sighed. "Insubordination, sir."

Chief Morgan nodded, pulled another file out of a pile and opened it. "You're a good officer. You work hard, take extra shifts, volunteer delivering food for the elderly during the holidays..." He pulled his finger down a page and flipped to the next, then the next. "So what happened?"

"I was out of line, sir," Gabe said quickly. If he could speed this along, he would. There was no need to convince Gabe of the error of his ways. He'd accepted that he should have handled this differently if he wanted to avoid this lovely autumnal two-week stay in the dullest town in Colorado. The changing leaves were beautiful this time of year, but he'd trade them for some Fort Collins city streets in a heartbeat.

"I want to know what actually happened," the chief said, meeting his gaze evenly. "I want your version."

Gabe cleared his throat. "Well, sir, my supervising officer ordered me to make an arrest, and I chose to let the perp go."

"And why would you defy an order?"

Why indeed? His supervising officer was a bully and had a personal vendetta against a twenty-year-old kid. The perp had bullied his supervisor's son in high school, and while Gabe could appreciate the seriousness of bullying, his supervisor's son wasn't exactly innocent, either. He was a twit who figured he could get away with anything because his dad was a cop.

"The perp was caught stealing baby clothes and diapers, sir," Gabe said. "I talked to him, and he said that his girlfriend needed some extra help in providing for their baby daughter. The perp and the girlfriend are no longer in a relationship, but he was trying to contribute—misguided as it might have been."

"So you felt sorry for him," the chief concluded.

"I recognized a spark of self-respect in the guy," Gabe replied. "And I didn't want to snuff it out."

"But it says here that when your supervising officer reprimanded you, that you…had words."

Gabe smiled grimly. That was putting it mildly. "That's the part I regret, sir. I should have kept my opinions about my supervising officer to myself."

"So what made you vent?"

Gabe paused, wondering how much he should say. The chief was regarding him with a look of sincere curiosity on his face.

"Between you and me, sir?" Gabe said. "The perp wasn't a complete unknown to my supervisor. He had gone to high school with my supervisor's son. The perp was a troublemaker from way back, but my supervisor's son wasn't exactly an innocent lamb, either. He's been let off with a warning for numerous infractions over the years because of his father's position. This one seemed… personal, I guess. And that wasn't fair. My supervisor's son is already off to college and he'll have a bright future despite his youthful mistakes because he got special treatment. The perp? At least he was trying to provide for his child. And by the way, I paid for the merchandise and recommended a warehouse that was hiring."

"Do you think he'll take you up on the sound advice?" Chief Morgan asked.

Gabe shrugged. "No idea. I wanted him to have the chance."

Chief Morgan nodded and made a few notes on his pad. "You were a bit of an underdog here in Comfort Creek when you were a kid, too, weren't you?"

"A bit," Gabe admitted.

"And do you think your issues with authority stem from that?"

Issues with authority… Okay, maybe he had a few. "No."

Chief Morgan laughed softly. "Tell me about your teenage years here in Comfort Creek."

"Not much to tell, sir."

Frankly, Gabe wasn't interested in talking about his personal history. He wasn't a problem to be fixed, and as the chief had pointed out, he had a pretty solid service record.

"I knew your grandmother," the chief added. "She was a good woman. I'm sorry for your loss."

His grandmother... She'd been the one to raise Gabe, and while he'd loved her, he'd hated her in equal measure. She'd been a bully, too, but she'd hidden it better. No one would believe that Imogen Banks, pillar of the church and knitter of baby booties, could have been a mean and spiteful woman in private. But she was, and her constant flow of cutting words had torn Gabe to shreds. Her passing didn't leave the hole in his heart that most people assumed.

"Thanks." It was the expected response, and he always provided it.

"So getting down to business, then," the chief went on. "I'm going to let you choose between two options. The first option is book work. In the basement, we have all sorts of binders with step-by-step lessons about dealing with our feelings in constructive manners. Or, we could do this another way."

Was there really a way to avoid the humiliating book work? He leaned forward and immediately regretted it. He didn't want to show weakness—an old habit that died hard.

"Is there another way, sir?" he asked hesitantly.

"Well...you could carry on doing patrol, keeping an eye on the bridal shop, and during the course of your stay here, you would record fifteen locations around town and your associations with them."

"My associations…" Gabe frowned.

"Memories." Chief Morgan leaned forward. "I want you to write down fifteen individual memories connected to fifteen individual locations in this community."

"That's rather personal, sir," Gabe replied.

"It is." The chief confirmed. "The thing is, Gabe, you're one of ours. You were raised in Comfort Creek, and I know that you're doing your very best to distance yourself from that fact. I have a feeling if you can make your peace with this town, and whatever it is that you hold against us, that your career will benefit."

"With all due respect, sir—" Gabe began, but the chief held up his hand and started reading from a page in front of him.

"'A bully. A twit. An overcompensating father making up for his pathetic son's inadequacies. A coward hiding behind a badge'…and a few more turns of phrase that you probably don't want to hear repeated." The chief looked up.

"Yeah…" Those had been his words, pretty much exactly.

"Are you sure all of that was referring to your supervisor?" the chief asked.

"I stand by them, sir," Gabe replied with a sigh.

The chief met his gaze for a moment and they regarded each other in silence. Then the chief shrugged. "Okay. So you prefer book work. I'm fine with that. I have your first binder set out downstairs."

Gabe scrubbed a hand through his mahogany curls. It was in his nature to balk at authority, and if the chief wanted him to take a different path, his first instinct was to put up a fight. But quite honestly, if he had to look down the barrel of two weeks in the precinct basement doing book work, or two weeks trying to track down Harper Kemp's robbers, he'd vastly prefer the latter.

"Sir, if it's all the same, I'd rather take your second option."

"Oh?" Chief Morgan raised his eyebrows. "All right then." He pulled out a small notebook and slid it across the desk. "In that case, this is for you."

Gabe picked it up and fanned the pages. It was empty.

"Thank you, sir."

"I'll leave you assigned to the bridal shop. We're all going to be keeping an eye on it, and the other local businesses if we're being targeted. I want you in plainclothes. We don't want to be too obvious."

"Will do." Gabe rose to his feet and tucked the notebook into his pocket.

"Welcome back," Chief Morgan said with a smile. "Wish it could have been more voluntary on your part, but we're glad to see you all the same."

"Thanks, sir." Gabe headed for the door. It was going to be a long two weeks.

Chapter Three

Harper bent over a dustpan and swept up the last of the glittering glass particles. At least she hoped this was the last of it. Every time she swept, she seemed to come up with more glass. At the counter, Zoey was drawing a picture and chattering to herself. Heidi had already left a few minutes earlier, leaving Harper and Zoey alone in the store.

The dress, newly pinned up and marked for Heidi's desired alterations, hung in the back room. Harper couldn't bring herself to touch it yet. The thought of shears slicing through the lace…it was almost physically painful. She'd talked Heidi down to knee length, which was something. Heidi had always liked being different—the girl with short hair when everyone else wore theirs long, a tattoo on her calf she liked to show off in summer, and very likely the reason she insisted upon a short dress for the wedding.

Couldn't Heidi, just once, blend in? Even if only for Chris!

A navy blue SUV rumbled to a stop outside. Harper paused and looked closer. Gabe got out, but he wasn't in uniform this time. He was wearing a pair of jeans and a gray T-shirt that tugged around his well-muscled biceps. Obviously, the police force kept him in shape, and she had to admit that Gabe had matured into a good-looking guy. A little less ruggedness would go a long way in making this more comfortable for her.

Harper met him at the door so she could unlock the deadbolt.

"Hi," Gabe said as she opened the door. She stepped back and he came inside.

"What happened to the uniform?" she asked.

"I'm supposed to blend in."

He didn't really succeed. Gabe was tall, muscled, and even in plainclothes, he looked like a brick wall. And maybe she liked that. If those thieves were going to return, she'd rather have Gabe as their distraction. Maybe they'd think twice and just move on.

Harper felt a tug on her hand and she glanced down to see Zoey looking up at Gabe, wide-eyed. Harper glanced between them, noting the similarities in their faces—the chin, the slate gray eyes... Did Gabe see it?

"This is Zoey," Harper said.

"Hi, Zoey." Gabe gave her a nod. "I'm Officer Banks."

That was formal, but what did Harper really expect? As far as he knew, this was his ex's daughter. Not his business.

"I drew a picture," Zoey said. She lifted it up for Gabe to see, and he took it from her fingers, regarded it for a moment.

"Very nice." He handed it back.

"It's for you," Zoey said.

"Oh—" Gabe's expression softened and he took the picture back. It wasn't much more than a few scribbles.

She was only four, after all. But he folded the paper in quarters and then tucked it into his back pocket. He cleared his throat. "Thank you, Zoey. I appreciate that."

Zoey seemed to like that, because she danced back to the counter to draw another one. Gabe would likely leave this shop with a whole ream of paper filled with Zoey's artwork, and right now he didn't even know how precious that was.

"You aren't used to kids, are you?" Harper asked as she leaned the broom into a corner.

"Not really," Gabe admitted. "But I am used to dealing with criminals and general run-of-the-mill bad guys, which you'll probably find more useful right about now."

Harper smiled ruefully.

"But you seem to have risen to the challenge," Gabe said.

"She was my goddaughter," Harper replied. "I've been in her life since birth."

"Seems like you've got it under control," he said with a nod. "So how've you been...otherwise, I mean?"

"I'm good." She glanced around. "I manage the store now. Dad had a hard time stepping down. This place was his heart and soul, you know? Anyway, he had a small stroke and that meant he had to slow down and recover."

"And you have your chance to run the place."

"Yeah. I've been waiting for this."

Gabe strolled across the store, his gaze moving over the window, the racks of dresses... He reached out, looking like he might finger the fabric of a gown, but instead he pushed it back and knocked on the wall behind.

"What are you looking for?" she asked.

"Don't know. Just looking." He shot her a wry smile. "So your dad's doing okay, though?"

"Yes, he's almost completely recovered, and he's settling into retirement with Mom. My sister's getting married."

"Yeah?" His gaze moved up to the ceiling, scanning from one side to the other. "Who'd she land?"

"Chris Holmes, of the Holmes Homes legacy."

"Ah—so she's marrying money."

"She's marrying a very decent man." Harper corrected him. "You'll probably see him around."

"Hmm." His gaze came back to Harper's face and he raised his eyebrows. "So…you still dislike me as much as you used to?"

"That's—" She felt the heat hit her face. "That was a long time ago, Gabe. I just thought that Andrea was expecting too much from you."

"So it was never personal," he said with an arched eyebrow. "Is that what you're saying?"

She sighed. "Maybe it was personal. If someone's against your relationship, it's hard not to be, right? So I'll take responsibility for that. I thought you would use my friend, and I didn't hide my opinion."

"I didn't use her."

"But you weren't good for her."

"Yeah, well, we might agree there," he said with a shrug. He turned away from her again and started scanning the store's floorboards. He was being thorough if nothing else. She couldn't help but follow his gaze, wondering what he was expecting to find.

"How does it feel to be home for a little while?" she asked after a few beats of silence.

"Awful."

She started to laugh, thinking he was joking, then she sobered. "What? Oh, you must mean with your grandmother's passing—"

Gabe walked away again, heading toward the counter. He peered into the back room, his head swiveling around to get a good look. When he remerged, his expression was different…gentler.

"Now that she's gone, I guess there's no harm in telling the truth," Gabe said. He turned his arm over and tapped a scar. "That was from her."

"What?" Harper looked closer—it was long and pale. He'd been cut deeply.

"She came at me when I'd been caught with a cigarette. I fell into some rocks."

Harper's mind reeled. "Wait… Came at you?"

"She wasn't the woman everyone thought she was," he said bitterly. "And I was a constant disappointment."

"Gabe, I had no idea…" Harper ran a hand over her brow. "Did you tell anyone?"

"Nope." Gabe shrugged. "We all have baggage. Mine is a little harder to set down, I guess."

"So being back here in Comfort Creek…it's not ideal," she clarified.

"You could say that."

"I'm sorry."

"Not your fault." He shot her a small smile. "It's just life."

It wouldn't be Zoey's life; that was for sure. Zoey would be loved and supported. She'd be appreciated, and when she was disciplined, it would be with gentle firmness. No child should have to live like that. It wasn't "just life." Harper sighed.

"Andrea told me that you didn't want kids. Was your grandmother part of that?"

He shot her a quirky smile. "Don't try to psychoanalyze me now, Harper."

"I'm not. I'm just curious. Like…if you'd somehow stumbled into parenthood, would that have been so bad?"

"Oh, like you did, you mean? Let's put it this way— I'm not anyone's first pick for godfather," he said with a chuckle. "I know better than to agree to those roles."

"No, I meant—" How could she even say this? It was delicate, and he wasn't making this any easier. How was it that Gabe hadn't pieced any of this together yet? Gabe raised an eyebrow and gave her a sardonic look.

"What if you'd gotten Andrea pregnant?" Harper asked, lowering her voice.

"I didn't."

"Just for argument's sake." Harper pressed, glancing over to where Zoey sat at the counter with her crayons, just to make sure they weren't overheard. "What if you had? Would you have just walked away?"

Gabe shook his head. "Look, Andrea and I weren't going to get married. I know she wanted all of that, and I really didn't. But it was more than that. She was a good woman, but she wasn't entirely right for me. So if you're thinking that we split up because of that alone—"

"No, no…" Harper heaved a sigh. "Let's put Andrea aside. What if you *did* have a child out there somewhere?"

"I don't know how to answer that," he said. "I don't tend to live my life by what-ifs. I'm a more pragmatic kind of guy. I'm not interested in the family life, and I take the necessary precautions. Or I did. I'm a Christian now, so I don't cross those lines anymore, and I don't play games. I don't toy with women's expectations. I put it out there pretty straight."

"Would you want to know about that child, though?" she pressed.

"Hypothetically, yeah. Sure." He eyed her curiously.

Zoey traipsed back across the room, a page fluttering in her grasp. It was just some swirls and dashes, but Harper knew the dedication her little girl put into those expressions of her feelings.

"It's for you," Zoey said, handing the picture up to Gabe with a proud smile. "It's a house. And a dog. And a sun. And another dog."

"Oh, very nice. Yes, I can see that clearly." Gabe looked at the page for a moment, then folded it and put into his back pocket with the other picture. "Thank you."

"Zoey, why don't you draw a picture for me?" Harper asked with a smile. "I love your pictures."

"Okay."

Zoey headed off again, leaving Harper and Gabe in relative privacy once more. She knew what she had to do here. The longer she put this off, the harder this conversation would be. But more than that—this was for Zoey. Her daughter would ask questions, and if Harper stood between Zoey and her biological father now, she knew who the bad guy would be—her. Gabe was in Comfort Creek, and deep in Harper's heart she sensed that there were more reasons to his arrival than just sensitivity training. God worked in weird ways, but it was always effective.

"Look, Andrea and I were over a long time ago,"

Gabe said. "I'm sorry that I was a disappointment to her, but that's all in the past."

"Yes, of course." Harper nodded. "I'm not trying to guilt you over the past. You two didn't work out, and that's not the end of the world. I'm asking because Andrea never told Zoey's father about her, and now that I'm her mom, I'm left in a bit of an ethical dilemma."

Gabe nodded. "So why didn't she tell him?"

"I think it was a complicated situation," Harper said delicately. "The relationship obviously didn't last, and she had…her own worries, I suppose. But she decided not to. And now that the adoption is underway, I don't want to do wrong by Zoey. I want to make sure that she has everything she needs, emotionally and physically, and I truly believe a little girl needs her daddy. I don't want to raise her so that my own heart is full, but hers has a hole in the size and shape of her father. When kids grow up with a hole in their hearts, they spend a lifetime trying it fill it, and it seldom works out well."

"Don't I know it," Gabe said softly.

His grandmother…she was still rolling that over in his mind. She'd never once suspected that Imogen Banks was anything less than the solid Christian woman she appeared to be.

"So do I tell him?" Harper asked. "That's my question. Do I tell the father that he has a child, even if that news wouldn't be welcome?"

Gabe was silent for a moment. "And you know this guy?"

"A little."

"I could do a background check on him, if you want. Just to make sure he's not…creepy, or something."

Harper laughed softly. "No, I don't think that's

necessary. He's a guy from town. So…not exactly a stranger."

"Oh. Well—" Gabe shrugged "—I'd tell him. At least he'd know, and you could tell Zoey that you did your best."

Tell him. She knew in her heart that she had to. Zoey's needs had to come first, and while Andrea had done her best by her daughter, Harper wasn't going to face God with Andrea, public opinion or her own excuses to back her up. She had to do the right thing.

"Besides," Gabe said with a slow smile, "you can rest easy that most guys aren't as messed up as I am."

"That doesn't really help." Harper licked her lips, closed her eyes for a moment in a fleeting prayer for guidance over her words, then blurted out, "Because Zoey's yours."

The smile slipped from Gabe's lips. *What?* He stared at Harper for a moment, processing her words. Or trying to. His mind wasn't reacting fast enough, and he found himself searching her expression for answers, instead of his own head. Her lips were parted as if she wanted to say more, then she pressed them shut. But those big green eyes stayed focused on him, her glasses seeming to magnify that clear gaze.

"No, she's not," he said at last. It seemed like a feeble thing to say, but everyone knew that Andrea had hooked up with another guy after she left him.

Harper glanced toward Zoey, and Gabe followed her gaze. The little girl was perched on a stool, her feet kicking in rhythmic thumps against the legs. She seemed totally preoccupied, hunched over a new picture at the counter.

"She is," Harper replied, her voice low. "If you look at Zoey's eyes—they're yours. And her chin—"

"A slight resemblance doesn't mean anything," he said with a short laugh. "A cleft in the chin isn't that rare, Harper."

"Andrea told me," Harper went on. "She lied to everyone about who the father was because she didn't want you to find out. The other guy was a cover story. You're Zoey's father, Gabe. I wouldn't have said anything if I wasn't sure."

Gabe sucked in a stabilizing breath. As a police officer, he was a critical judge of people's stories. How many times had a perp pleaded his innocence, only to have all the evidence on him? How many men in prison claimed to be innocent? Almost all of them. He knew what a lie sounded like, and he heard the truth in her voice.

"So I'm the guy that Andrea thought was no good for Zoey?" he said after a moment.

Harper's silence was all the answer he needed, and that confirmation was like a punch to the gut. They'd made a baby... When he'd been promising himself that he'd stop crossing that line with her, that he'd get his head straight and stop fooling around... When he'd been wondering if it wasn't just better to break up considering that they wanted such different things... While he hadn't been man enough to just do what he knew he had to do, they'd made a baby.

He'd never guessed.

Andrea had been the one to break it off with him, and he'd known she was right. But when she'd walked away, she'd been pregnant, and that changed the way he saw himself. He was no longer a guy who knew better than to shackle a woman down to the likes of him. He was now the guy that his pregnant girlfriend had run away from.

Gabe had never claimed to be father material—or even husband material, for that matter—but to have a woman actively hide his child from him…

A father. That's what this kept coming back to. He was a father?

His gaze moved back toward Zoey, who was climbing down from her stool again, a piece of paper clutched in one hand. He was looking at her differently this time, scanning her small, round face for signs of his own. His hand moved up to his own chin, rubbing against that familiar cleft under the sandpaper of stubble, and his mind was spinning in a fog of shock.

"Look!" Zoey said, holding up the paper to Harper. "I drew all of us. That's Mommy, and Mommy, and me and Grandma and Grandpa…and that's a cricket."

Harper's eyes misted and she nodded, then kissed Zoey's head. "I love it," she said. "Your snack is in my bag. It's on the desk in the back room. Why don't you go get it?"

Zoey skipped off, and Harper looked down at the faint scribbles on the page.

"Mommy and Mommy," Harper said. "That's what she calls me and Andrea. I've been upgraded to Mommy, recently, but when she tells stories, you have to know which Mommy she's talking about."

Gabe watched Zoey go—sturdy little legs and tangled brown waves. His emotions hadn't caught up to this yet, and so far, she just looked like a kid—not *his* kid, not someone any closer to him than any other kid was… But when Harper looked at Zoey, he could see love burning deep in those green eyes. She saw something more when she looked at that child...

Gabe scrubbed a hand through his brown curls. "So Andrea knew she was pregnant when she left."

"Yes." Harper turned back toward him. "She said that she knew you didn't want to get married or have kids, and once she realized she was pregnant, she knew that she had to make her choices with a child in mind, too. And she couldn't keep doing...whatever it was you two were doing. The back and forth. The constant trying. So she came home."

Home. That was Comfort Creek for Andrea, but this town wasn't home for him. He'd been determined never to return to this hypocritical town. It had an attractive enough veneer, but he knew what was burbling underneath...and suddenly a thought struck him for the very first time.

"And no one told me."

"Andrea made me promise to keep the secret," Harper said.

"And you're the only one who knew? I'm sure her parents knew I was the father. And her brother would have known, too, I imagine. If they knew, there would have been others—aunts and uncles, close friends, *promising to keep that secret*."

Pink rose in Harper's cheeks. "I told you."

"She's four." He couldn't mask the edge in his tone. "It's been five years."

"She wasn't my daughter then," Harper retorted. "And it wasn't my business."

Yeah, that's what everyone in this town said about his grandmother, too. The way she raised her grandson was none of their business. What she did behind closed doors was her personal business, and far be it from them to push into someone else's privacy. She was old, and he was a handful—they could sympathize with poor Imogen. But never once did they question whether Gabe's behavioral issues might have arisen because of his crotchety old grandmother.

Gabe had been a little boy who was told how terrible he was on a daily basis. He'd been an adolescent hiding the emotional bruises from his grandmother's caustic comments. And now most recently, he was the father of a daughter he didn't even know existed. Not deemed good enough by Andrea and those closest to her. Ironically, that wasn't very different from his grandmother.

This town had clean streets and cordial smiles, like the one from Chief Morgan, and under it all was the cesspool of secrets. He had a little girl, and Comfort Creek had kept its collective mouth shut. This stupid town hadn't changed a bit.

"Not your business." He nodded slowly. "I *should* have known about her, and long before this."

Harper nodded and tugged her ginger curls away from her face. "I agree. But I'm telling you now."

"And if it hadn't been for that car accident?" he prodded. If Andrea hadn't died, leaving her daughter...*their* daughter...in Harper's care, what then?

Harper shrugged faintly. "What would you have had me do, Gabe? Go behind my best friend's back and inform you about Zoey? I couldn't do that. But I was the voice of reason and balance. I encouraged her to tell you, and eventually...I think she would have."

"When Zoey was a teenager?" he asked.

"I thought you didn't work with what-ifs?" She looked away.

So, he'd hit a nerve, had he? Good—she deserved to

squirm a little bit. This whole town did! His emotions were kicking in now, and it wasn't the appropriate emotional response…not what people expected to see when a man discovered he had a child. He wasn't overflowing with love. He wasn't feeling tender and paternal.

"This town." His voice trembled with barely restrained anger. "Everyone keeps their secrets, don't they? They close the circle and claim to be so innocent. But what happens when they close the circle and you're the one on the outside? Huh? I was raised in Comfort Creek since my mother dumped me with my grandmother shortly after my birth. Chief Morgan just gave me a very touching speech saying that I'm one of your own. But this town didn't take care of me. And one day, it might not take care of you, either."

"So you wanted to know." Harper shook her head. "Andrea didn't think you would! If you had any kind of flexibility, maybe you should have let Andrea know that, because I'm not taking responsibility for—"

Zoey appeared in the doorway, and as Gabe's gaze landed on the girl, the words died in Harper's mouth.

"We shouldn't discuss any of this in front of her," Harper said, her voice tight.

"Yeah. Agreed." Even he could see that their old, festering issues would be poison for that little girl.

Zoey stared at them, gray eyes wide. Did Zoey have any sense of who he was? When he was a boy, he used to imagine that his dad would come back for him. His mom was a lost cause, but he'd held out hope for a dad. He'd figured that he'd know his dad right away—some sort of innate feeling, or something. But that had only been a childhood fantasy. In reality, it was possible to look your own child in the face and have no idea who she was.

"Zoey, it's okay, sweetheart," Harper said, her tone softening. "Come here. We're done talking about that anyway."

"Are you fighting like with Aunt Heidi?" Zoey asked doubtfully.

"Yes." Shame clouded her expression. "Something like that. But we won't anymore."

Gabe had to get out of here. He needed space to process all of this, and he didn't trust himself to do it in front of Zoey.

"I'm going to head out." He hooked a thumb over his shoulder. "I'll be in touch."

It was too casual of a statement to encompass it all, but he didn't know how to deal with this—and his anger wasn't going to be of use right now. He needed space.

Before Harper could say anything, he marched to the door and pulled it open. Outside that door was freedom, but something tugged his gaze back over his shoulder once more to the curly redhead who stared at him with regret swimming in her eyes and the dark-haired child next to her, an apple slice held aloft.

He'd promised himself that he'd never come back to this town for good reason, but that was before he'd known he had a child here, and all of his issues aside, life had just gotten a hundred percent more complicated.

"I'll be back," he said, moderating his tone. He wasn't sure why he said it. Maybe it was because of their stricken expressions, or because he knew that he owed that child something more than DNA, whether he liked it or not.

Then he pushed out onto the sidewalk and pulled the door solidly shut behind him.

Chapter Four

Harper hadn't handled that very well, had she? Or maybe it was just Gabe who hadn't taken the news very gracefully. It wasn't like she'd had a lot of time to plan it out. If she'd waited and told him another time—maybe when he was back in Fort Collins—there would always be the question of why she hadn't told him *now*. This was the right thing…wasn't it? How much gentler could she have been?

Regardless, Gabe had run for the hills, and she wasn't surprised. At least she shouldn't be.

Harper finished dismantling the mannequins that had been slashed—she couldn't look at those demolished dresses any longer. They were expensive gowns, and while insurance would compensate her for her loss, it wasn't only about the money. The vandalism was violent, frightening and such a willful destruction of something beautiful. She took some photos for insurance purposes and then folded what was left of the gowns into storage boxes. Maybe she could make use of some of the fabric for something else and they wouldn't be a complete waste.

Harper kept looking up whenever she heard a noise, expecting to see Gabe come back in, but he didn't return. Zoey finished drawing her pictures, and when Harper was convinced she wouldn't get anything more done with her daughter underfoot, she locked up the shop and drove Zoey home.

Harper didn't live far from the shop. Her house was a little two-bedroom bungalow two streets over from where she'd grown up. It was the perfect-size home for a woman on her own, so bringing Zoey into the mix had required some reshuffling—of everything. What used to be her home office was now Zoey's bedroom. It was just as well, Harper decided. Now that she had a child to care for, she'd leave work at work. There was no more room for it in her evenings with Zoey.

"Will we get the crowns back?" Zoey asked, kicking off her shoes. Harper caught the girl's jacket before it hit the ground and hung it on the peg behind her.

"Probably not," Harper said. "But the insurance company will give us money to order more."

"I miss the crowns."

So did Harper. This robbery felt personal. It was an invasion, and it had left her more shaken than she liked to admit.

"Are you hungry?" Harper asked.

"Yep. Can I have a snack?" Zoey asked hopefully. "I want cheese."

"I'll make supper," Harper replied with a rueful shake of her head. "And after supper, you're going to visit Grandma Jane for a little while. She's going to make cookies with you."

"Cookies?"

"You know Grandma Jane's cookies." She smiled.

"Mommy made good cookies…"

There it was—the sadness that always seemed so close to the surface, and Harper sank down onto her haunches and opened up her arms. "Come here, sweetie."

Zoey crawled into Harper's arms and she held the girl close, breathing in the scent of her. This child had lost so much, and Harper couldn't make it okay. All she could do was hug her through it.

"I miss your mom, too," Harper said softly. "Her cookies were great, weren't they?"

Zoey nodded mutely against Harper's shoulder.

"And we'll see her again, Zoey," Harper murmured. "One day, when we're in Heaven. That wasn't a forever goodbye, sweetie. That was a…so long for now."

That's when Harper would have to hand Zoey back to Andrea and tell her that she'd done her very best to raise Zoey right and to keep Andrea's memory alive. It was a mammoth job, and she was only now starting to appreciate how hard it would be.

Harper's legs began to cramp, and she laughed softly. "I'm going to fall over, Zoey."

Zoey giggled and wriggled free as Harper caught herself with one hand, and Zoey wandered off to the living room. Thankfully, Harper wasn't completely alone in this. She had the grandparents—Andrea's parents and her own—who were a wealth of advice, babysitting and prayer. Plus there was her sister, friends and community… Harper would take all the help she could get.

Supper that night consisted of chicken nuggets, mashed potatoes and some boiled carrots on the side. Boiled carrots were one of the few vegetables that Zoey would eat without too much complaint. One of the things Harper had learned over the last six months was that Zoey was capable of living entirely off snack food if allowed, and it was up to Harper to insist upon meals three times a day. Cheese sticks, applesauce cups and fish-shaped crackers did not make for balanced nutrition. Most days. Some days, she chose her battles.

And speaking of battles, today she'd chosen a doozy telling Gabe about his daughter. Thinking about it now, she should have talked to Andrea's parents, Mike and Jane Murphy, first. They'd certainly have a few opinions about what she'd just done, and she honestly wasn't sure if she'd have their support in this.

"Lord, what was I thinking?" she breathed.

Harper rubbed her hands over her face. She wouldn't rest tonight—not while she was wondering how Gabe had taken all of this. She had three options: talk to the Murphys and see how they reacted, talk to Gabe and see what he was feeling, or…wait.

Waiting wasn't actually an option—who was she kidding? Since Zoey was scheduled to hang out with her grandparents this evening, she might as well make use of the time to herself and get things sorted out with Gabe. The Murphys would have questions—lots of them—and she'd rather have a few answers lined up.

So that evening, after dropping Zoey off with the Murphys, Harper drove to the police station and parked. The station glowed from the inside, and Harper eyed the brick building uncertainly. If Gabe was working, she wasn't going to be a welcome sight.

"Whatever," she muttered aloud.

Harper got out of her vehicle and headed up the walk to the front door. So he wouldn't be thrilled to see her… She shouldn't have to chase the man down, either! He'd just been told that he was a father, not that he was dying.

Any man should be honored to be Zoey's dad. She was a smart, sweet little girl with a heart of gold, and acknowledging her wasn't a punishment. So let him be uncomfortable—she was in Zoey's court right now, and she was doing this for her daughter.

Harper trotted up the front steps and pulled open the glass door. A welcome wave of warmth hit her as she stepped inside the precinct. She rubbed her hands together and paused at the empty reception desk. She glanced at her watch—it was almost seven o'clock, and the receptionist would have already gone home. So she headed over to the bull pen and peered inside.

Bryce Camden was sitting at his desk, typing at his computer. He glanced up when he saw her. There wasn't anyone else around that Harper could see.

"Hi," Bryce said. "Can I help you?"

"Yes, I was looking for one of the visiting officers—Gabe Banks."

"He's here," Bryce replied. He looked toward a hallway, then around the office. "I'm just finishing something up here. He's in the lunchroom on break. You could just poke your head in there—it wouldn't be a problem."

Harper hesitated, then sighed. What other option did she have? At least there wasn't an audience for this meeting. She headed toward the closed door Bryce indicated, and looked back to get his confirmation it was the right room. Then she tapped on the door and pushed it open.

Gabe wasn't alone in the room as expected, and Harper stopped short. There was a woman with him, and Gabe was leaning on the edge of a counter, facing her. His warm gaze was locked on her face, and he

was laughing softly about something. The woman—
Harper recognized her as an officer, but she wasn't in
uniform—was staring at him adoringly.

Yeah—not much had changed around here. Harper
felt a rise of anger that she couldn't quite explain. What
should it matter to her if he was flirting around town
again?

"Sorry to interrupt," Harper said curtly, and both
Gabe and the woman turned toward her.

"Not at all," she said. "My shift is over anyway. I'd
better get home." The woman rose to her feet and leaned
in, kissing Gabe on the cheek. "You're one in a million,
Gabe. You know that, right?"

"Of course," Gabe said with a playful shrug. "But
it's nice to hear all the same."

"You…" The woman shook her head. "Good night.
I'm going home."

"Good night, Tammy."

Tammy nodded to Harper as she headed out of the
room, and Harper stared at Gabe in mild disgust. It
didn't take him long to work the field, did it? She didn't
know why this bothered her so much—because she was
being proven right, after all—but it did.

"What are you doing here?" Gabe asked, and Harper
raised an eyebrow. He frowned. "What?"

"Same old Gabe Banks," she said, wishing she
sounded a little less bitter than she did.

"That?" He hooked a thumb toward the half-open
door. "First of all, you don't have a right to question
anything I do. Second, don't judge a situation before
you know what's going on."

"I'm not asking," Harper replied. "You're right. Not
my business."

Gabe eyed her for a moment, then sighed. "I should have come back into the store."

"Yes, you should have." But coming here had been a mistake. She could feel it already. These were his stomping grounds, not hers, and she'd probably see more than she wanted to. Gabe might be Zoey's dad, but he wasn't anything more to Harper, so she'd better start appreciating those boundaries now.

"I was around, you know," he said. "I didn't just leave you there without police supervision."

"That would have been nice to know," she said.

"I'm sorry if you felt...unsafe." His voice lowered. "I was there. I'm not proud of how I handled that, and I think I owe you an apology."

There was his charm again—but charm wasn't going to be enough here.

"It's okay. I get that I dropped a bomb on you. I came by tonight because I was worried." She glanced in the direction Tammy had left. "Although I probably shouldn't have bothered."

A humored smile tickled his lips. "I'm a big boy now, Harper."

"Actually, I was more worried about Zoey," she retorted. "Obviously, you can fend for yourself. You always have."

Gabe ignored the inference and sighed. "Did you tell Zoey about me? I'd assumed you wouldn't—not yet, at least."

"No, no, I haven't told her," Harper replied. "But this does concern her, doesn't it? You're her father, and if you don't want to be in her life, I can live with that." In some selfish part of her heart, she might even be hoping for it, she realized. "But I need to know where you stand on all of this."

Gabe glanced at his watch. "Would you mind going outside to talk about this? This is kind of private."

"Oh—" Harper nodded. He didn't seem to mind if people saw him flirting with Officer Tammy... She tried to push that thought away. "Sure. Let's go outside."

Gabe led the way, and as they passed Bryce, he gave them a friendly nod. Gabe pulled on a jacket and Harper tugged hers a little closer as they stepped outside in the brisk chill. Gabe held the door for her, and she tried to ignore just how tall and broad he was. This wasn't her residual attraction to him, and she needed to keep her head on straight.

The moon hung low in the sky, and Harper could smell smoke from a fireplace surfing the breeze. Gabe led the way to a bench that faced the street and he sat down. Harper sat next to him, squeezing her knees together.

"Okay, I guess I should start by saying that I've been thinking about Zoey all day," he said, "and the thing I keep coming back to is that Andrea didn't want me to even know about this kid."

Harper had always thought that was a mistake, but now she could appreciate her friend's position a little better. To be in love with that man and watch him move on with other women—it would have been painful.

"That's in the past," she said. "I'm her mom, now."

"Except you weren't so wrong about me," Gabe said, his voice low. "I'm one of those messed-up guys who looks good on paper but has too many issues to be the kind of rock a woman needs. When Andrea found out she was pregnant, where did she go?"

"Home," Harper murmured.

"To *you*." Gabe looked over at her. "Am I right?"

"I was her best friend."

"And I was her boyfriend. I was the *father*." He shook his head. "But you saw that all along, didn't you?"

Harper licked her lips as a chill breeze whisked her red curls into her eyes. She pulled her hair back. "I admit, I wasn't a big champion of your relationship, and that was mainly because of the guy you were when I knew you—here in town. You were a womanizer. A flirt. You didn't take anything seriously."

"I was a kid with a lot of problems. You were right to see through my tough act. I wish more people had."

His voice was low, and something warm sparkled in his dark eyes. He met her gaze easily and she felt something inside of her soften in spite of her best intentions.

"How do you do that?" Harper asked suddenly.

"What?" He eyed her uncertainly.

"I just watched you flirting shamelessly with that officer in there, and you turn around the next minute and make me feel like—" She stopped. She was saying too much already.

"Like what?" he pressed, that warm gaze still fixed on her.

"Like you see me. Like I'm important. Like I'm the only woman in this town. It's a nice trick. You're very good at it."

"Flirting?" He barked out a laugh. "That's what you thought that was? I'll tell you something, Harper. When I'm flirting with you, you'll know it."

She felt heat creep into her cheeks. "You're doing it again."

"Sorry." He shot her an impish smile. "It's just that I

wasn't flirting. I did her a favor. She was grateful. Not that it's your business, but I helped her contact her little sister who'd run away and landed in Fort Collins. She hadn't seen her in five years, and she *was* grateful."

"Oh." Harper felt a little bad knowing that. "Grateful enough to kiss you, it seems."

"Apparently." He shot her an irritated look. "I didn't ask for that. You act like I'm angling for female attention around here, and that's the last thing I'm doing. So when I'm uncomfortable, I put on that act—pretend that I'm all cocky and confident. It doesn't mean I feel it—it just means I'm trying to smooth over an uncomfortable situation. It's not like I'm married."

No, it wasn't. Harper sighed and looked away. It shouldn't matter. This wasn't about the character traits she liked in men. And as he pointed out, he was very, very single right now. She was here for her daughter, and she had to remember that.

"So where does this leave Zoey?" Harper asked.

Gabe was silent for a moment. "What are you wanting from me? Are you asking me to take my daughter with me back to Fort Collins—"

"No!" Harper couldn't help the passion in the word and she lowered her voice again, not wanting it to carry. "No. Andrea left Zoey to me because I've been her godmother since birth. I love Zoey with all my heart, and I have no desire to give her up. I just happen to know that a little girl needs her dad, too."

"She needs a good dad, not just a biological one," he replied, his voice so quiet that the chilled breeze almost whisked his words away.

"You're all she's got," Harper countered.

"I only found out about her this morning." Gabe met

her gaze solemnly. "And I'm back in town because I'm being disciplined for my problems with authority. So I'm not exactly in a good place."

"All right. Fair enough." Harper pulled her keys from her pocket. Even the little bit she was hoping for seemed to be asking too much.

"Hey." His deep voice tugged her gaze back upward, and he met it levelly. "I didn't want marriage and children. That's still true, but I have good reason for that. It isn't selfish. I mean, who doesn't want a woman to call his own, kids to love? But a family needs more than I can offer, and instead of setting myself up for divorce after divorce, instead of disappointing woman after woman and setting kids up for a lifetime of disillusionment because I wasn't enough, I'm being honest with myself."

"I'm not here to judge—" she began.

"Aren't you?" he quipped. "You sure jumped to a few conclusions inside there."

Harper clenched her jaw and dropped her gaze.

"And I guess that's okay," Gabe conceded with a sigh. "You're Zoey's mom, now, and judging the people you let into her life is pretty much your job."

Harper nodded slowly. "Okay. So maybe I'm judging a little bit."

"Here's the thing," Gabe said. "I know where my strengths lie, and it isn't in the family life. But I'm also not the same guy I was five years ago."

"No?" He could have fooled her.

"I'm a Christian now, for one," he said. "I don't chase women anymore—that's over. But faith in God doesn't change who I am, and my own garbage that I have to sort through. It just gives me some divine guidance

while I do it. But that said, I'm a father. That's a biological fact, and I don't want to let Zoey down."

"That's a good thing," Harper replied. "Because even
if Zoey hasn't thought to ask about you yet, she will as
she gets older. She'll need to know about you—you're
a part of her."

The most Harper hoped for right now was that Gabe
would be a decent father—from a distance. That he'd
remember Zoey's birthdays and visit her a few times a
year. That he'd Skype with her from time to time and
make her feel like she mattered to him without this dis-
tressingly attractive man actually getting underfoot here
in Comfort Creek.

And the realization stabbed some guilt deep inside of
her. Zoey deserved better, and Harper's feelings toward
Gabe shouldn't matter one bit in that equation. *Please
God, let him not disappoint his daughter too deeply.*

Gabe looked at Harper, her curls ruffling in the cold
wind. The tip of her nose was pink, and she glanced
at him, green eyes glittering in suppressed emotion.
Obviously, Harper still didn't have an incredibly high
opinion of him, and he was already kicking himself
for that. He fell back into old habits—acting smoother
than he felt when it came to women. He knew how to
charm them, and he didn't want to be that guy anymore, but he'd managed to back himself into that corner all over again with Tammy. At least when it came
to appearances.

Harper was the one who'd never seen much use in
him, and the woman who had enticed him from the
start. Somehow, facing all of this with Harper seemed
to set him at an emotional disadvantage.

"How should we do this?" she asked, breaking the silence.

"I'll be sending you child support payments," Gabe said. "You don't have to worry about chasing me down for that."

"I appreciate that, but that isn't what I meant. I'm not worried about the money."

He reached into his back pocket and pulled out the folded picture Zoey had made for him. He tapped it against his palm a couple of times. "To start, I think I should meet my daughter—properly, I mean."

It felt strange to refer to "his daughter," words that had never entered his mind in the past. He was a dad… or maybe not exactly a *dad*. Dads were there for their kids—they'd earned the title. Like Bryce adopting that little girl with his wife. Bryce was a dad; Gabe was at most a biological father.

"You don't like me much," Gabe said. "But maybe we can sort out some kind of friendship between us."

She didn't counter him, but after a beat of silence, she said, "Why don't you come for dinner tomorrow evening? It will give me some time to talk to Zoey and explain it all to her."

"I, uh—" He looked up, catching her eye. "Harper, I'm not good with kids, and I don't have anyone else to turn to. I might need some help in…I don't know… connecting with her."

She softened, then shrugged weakly. "I'll pitch in."

"Thanks." That did make it feel a bit easier. "So what time should I come over…six?"

"Yes, that would be fine." She opened her purse and rummaged through it, pulling out a piece of paper and a pen. She jotted something down and handed it over. "My phone number and address."

Gabe accepted the paper, tore a strip off the bottom, then plucked the pen from her soft fingers with a half smile. Her cheeks colored ever so slightly, and she dropped her gaze. He jotted down his own phone number and handed both the pen and the paper back to her.

"That's my cell phone number. Better than dropping in on me at work."

"Thank you." The blush in her cheeks deepened.

"Can I bring anything?" he asked.

"No, no. I'll have dinner sorted out," she replied. Behind her, a whirl of wind picked up a scattering of leaves and spun them across the grass. His emotions did a similar tumble inside of his gut.

"I want you to know that I love her, Gabe," Harper went on. "My heart has already closed around her. Do you get that?"

Was she afraid that if he got to know his daughter, he'd try to take her away? Harper was risking a lot by telling him about Zoey, and in that moment he could sense how much was on the line with doing the right thing. She was a better person than he was.

"Look, Harper," Gabe said slowly. "I'm not exactly great single-father material. I'm not interested in tearing Zoey out of her home. I just figure I should meet her. That's all. No pressure."

Harper let out a silent sigh. "That's good to hear. Thank you, Gabe."

A thought occurred to him—he'd need to bring Zoey something, a gift of some sort. Wasn't that what guilty, absentee fathers did?

"Harper, what sorts of things does a four-year-old girl like?" he asked suddenly.

"Right now, she's all about princesses."

"So typical girl stuff." Maybe this wouldn't be so hard after all. He'd just head to the pink aisle in Walmart.

"No, not just girl stuff." Harper's tone sharpened. "Princesses, specifically. She was really upset that the tiaras were taken from my store. She loved trying them on. And the plastic ones don't cut it. She's experienced Swarovski crystals, and there is no going back."

"Ah."

"And she likes tools—hammers, drills, you name it."

"Seriously?" He squinted at her, unsure if she was joking.

"She's a whole little person, Gabe. You have a lot to catch up on."

Apparently so. He'd asked for her help, and she was providing it. "Tools. Tiaras. Got it."

"Okay." She rose to her feet and dug her keys out of her pocket. "See you tomorrow."

Harper didn't wait for his farewell, and she headed across the grass toward the parking lot through a drift of crunching leaves. He tore his eyes away from her, trying to quell that strange, rising warmth inside of him when he looked at her.

He needed to stick to the task at hand: finding his daughter a present that she'd like. Tomorrow was Sunday, and while he had no intention of attending church here in Comfort Creek, he wasn't exactly free, either. There was a store to watch, just in case the crooks came back to take advantage of the town's day of rest.

He couldn't show up tomorrow night empty-handed.

But what was supposed to make up for a lifetime of silence? And just how resentful would that little girl be?

Gabe looked down at the faint scribbles on the page. What had she said she'd drawn? He couldn't remember now. He hadn't been paying attention. She'd just been Andrea's kid…and now she was so much scarier—she was a little girl with every right to hate him.

Gabe looked back toward Harper's car as the engine revved to life. Her car pulled away from the curb, and he watched the taillights disappear around the corner at the stop sign. The chill of the autumn evening tugged him out of his thoughts and he headed back into the station. His life would never be the same again—he could already feel it. And Harper made all of this harder still. If only Zoey's new mom could be a woman he felt nothing for. That would make it easier. When he let her down, he wouldn't feel like such a failure.

Zoey had a mom to love her—Gabe had never had that luxury. His mom had dumped him on his grandmother's doorstep and come by to see him once every couple of years. She'd bring an age-inappropriate birthday gift and drink a beer while staring at him dismally. Gabe was her greatest regret—she'd told him that one year, and then hadn't explained the statement. Just let it hang there. Then she'd driven off again and disappeared until his high school graduation when she showed up with some stringy-haired boyfriend and a bottle of tequila that was supposed to be his grad gift. Still age-inappropriate. He'd only been eighteen.

"You turned out good," she'd said with an overflow of mascara-running emotion. "You're a grown man now. Look at you! I can't believe I'm your mama!"

But she wasn't his "mama." She was his biological

mother. He'd never had a "mama" in his life. Zoey had that kind of love—Harper, who knew the things she liked, the things she didn't... Who stood up for her, fought for her. *That* was a mother.

Mom's boyfriend drank the bottle of tequila after Gabe's graduation was complete, which was just as well, looking back on it. The last thing Gabe had needed was alcohol in the mix.

After that last visit at his graduation, Grandma hadn't bothered getting nasty. Instead, she'd sat him down and said, "Gabriel, my job is done. I think you'll agree that I've done my due diligence with you. Time to get a full-time job and your own place. You have one month, and then I want you out. This is for your own good." Then she'd added after a moment of awkward silence, "I've prayed on it."

At the time, he'd found that ironic, but those words still stewed in a raw, angry part of his heart. Maybe she did pray, but he doubted that her prayers went any further than the ceiling. If she'd connected to God, Gabe figured he'd see some of that Christian love the preacher went on and on about in church every Sunday. There was a story that Jesus told about how some people would say, "Lord, Lord," and God would reply, "I never knew you." Wasn't that the parable? Gabe might have been messed up and angry, but he knew his Bible well enough to use it as a weapon when he argued with his grandmother. If Grandma had ever truly known God, that would be a surprise to him.

Was Gabe supposed to write down *that* memory, too? He touched the notebook in his breast pocket. He was too tired to play along with the chief's training right now. He heaved a sigh and headed for the station.

As Gabe came inside, he saw Bryce at the coffeepot, arms crossed over his chest as he watched it drip.

"Hey, man," Gabe said. "Where do you buy toys in this town?"

"Toys?" Bryce frowned. "Why?" Then a smile spread over his face. "Harper Kemp—you're not trying to soften her up, are you?"

"No." Gabe's first instinct was to keep his personal business private, but how long would this paternity stay a secret anyway? "Look, it's still pretty delicate," Gabe confessed. "This has nothing to do with Harper…directly, at least. I found out today that I'm the father of Andrea Murphy's daughter."

Bryce stared at him for a moment. "Wait…what?"

"Yeah, that was my first response, too," Gabe replied wryly. "But I need to bring her something tomorrow night. Harper is going to tell her who I am, and I'm going over there for dinner."

If he arrived empty-handed, he'd just be the joker who'd never been around. If he came with the right gift, maybe he could distract the kid from the disappointment of who he was.

"Okay…" Bryce eyed Gabe uncertainly. "Everything's closed Sunday. Here in town, at least. I mean, I guess you could drive to Fort Collins for the Walmart."

"I thought of that, but I can't go to Fort Collins," Gabe replied. "It's a day off of sensitivity training, but I'm keeping an eye on Harper's store in case the thieves return."

"I don't know if it's the kind of toy a little girl would like, but I picked up a pair of toy handcuffs the other week for my nephew, but then I didn't see him—if you want them," Bryce offered.

"Yeah, thanks. That would help."

Handcuffs. Hey, if the kid liked hammers, maybe she'd see the allure of a set of cuffs, too.

"No problem." The coffeepot stopped burbling, and Bryce poured himself a mug. He lifted the pot in a silent offer and Gabe nodded.

"Sure, I'll take a cup." Gabe sighed. "I honestly had no idea I'd fathered that little girl, and I have no idea what I'm doing. I'm not the dad type, poor kid."

"You'll figure it out." Bryce filled another mug and passed it to Gabe. "I didn't think I was ready to be a dad, either. But you settle in more easily than you think."

Gabe nodded slowly. "I hope so."

"You want to know the secret?" Bryce asked, crossing his arms over his chest. "You fall in love with them, and that's the clincher. You realize that you'd do anything for them, just to make sure they have the best life possible. That's a dad's job, isn't it—provide the best?"

And maybe he would settle in, except Gabe hadn't felt anything at all when he met his daughter the first time. Granted, he hadn't known she was his, but still… he should have felt something, shouldn't he? This ridiculously quiet town had just turned into a whole lot more than some book work about feelings and how to respond appropriately. It was now a whole lot worse…

He'd never been good enough for a woman like Harper. What made anyone think he had anything to offer his daughter?

Chapter Five

"You *told* him?" Jane Murphy gasped.

Harper stood in the Murphys' kitchen, her arms crossed protectively over her chest. Jane Murphy stared at Harper, her lipsticked lips parted in an expression of dismay. Her elegant gray hair was tucked behind her ears, and she wore a gray cardigan that perfectly matched her tresses, but the expression of pure shock on her face left Harper's mouth dry. This was the exact response she'd been worried about.

"I had to," Harper said. "He's Zoey's father. He needed to know about her."

Mike Murphy sat at the kitchen table, and he stared down at a coffee mug so hard that Harper half expected it to crack under his glare. He didn't look up, and instead chewed the side of his cheek. Out in the living room, Zoey was asleep on the couch. Still, they were all trying to keep their voices down.

"You know how he treated Andrea!" Jane turned her back and stalked to the fridge, then turned back. "He crushed her. You know better than anyone! She loved that man, and she was never enough for him."

"I know," Harper said quickly. "And while we love Andrea still, this is about Zoey and what she needs."

"You think he'll do better by his daughter than he did by ours?" Mike said, speaking for the first time. He raised his driving gaze up to meet Harper's.

"At the moment, Zoey doesn't have a dad in her life," Harper replied. "Or a living mother. She has me, grandparents who adore her, and she has some extended family. So far, she's too young to take much notice. She's still grieving for her mom. But one of these days, she's going to start asking questions about her father. This isn't avoidable."

"She could choose if she wanted to contact him herself," Mike retorted. "When she's older."

"After denying her a father for all those years?" Harper couldn't back down on this one. "I had my dad growing up, and he and I are really close. A father-daughter relationship is important to a girl. You should know—Andrea had *you*, and you were her strength when life kicked her down. You were there for her every step of her childhood, and when she got pregnant, she knew where to turn."

"Because I was man enough!" Mike snapped. "A real man sticks with it. He commits. This Gabe twit—"

"I don't know what kind of father Gabe will make," Harper said quickly. "I'm not guaranteeing anything with this man. But she at least needs to know him. Even if just to take away the mystery. Do we want her to grow up imagining some knight on a white horse? She'll hate us for keeping him away. It might be better to let her see the reality of her father for herself."

"And if he breaks Zoey's heart, too?" Mike asked.

"Then she'll have all of us to help her to make sense

of it," Harper replied. "Besides, I'll be there—supervising everything. If I think it isn't healthy for Zoey, I'll put a stop to it."

"What did he say?" Jane asked, her voice trembling. "When you told him he was a father, what did he say? Exactly."

"Well, he was shocked."

"What did he *say*?" Jane pressed.

"Well, he left the store to go think it over," Harper replied slowly. "And I went down to the station to talk to him—"

"So he didn't call you. You had to go find him," Mike clarified. "He ran off."

This wasn't looking good for Gabe and Harper shrugged weakly. "He said that he wants to know her."

"Does that mean he wants custody?" Jane's voice was tight. "He could decide that he wants to raise Zoey himself. You realize that, don't you? He's her biological dad, and with Andrea gone, he's her only living parent."

"No. He was clear about that. He's not going to try to take her away from us. He just…really at this point, he just wants to meet her."

"Isn't he in town under disciplinary action?" Mike asked.

"Yes, he is." Harper nodded. "Sensitivity training, like the rest of them."

"And this is the father you want in her life?" he asked dejectedly.

"It isn't about *my* choice," Harper replied, irritation starting to simmer. "He's her father! What can I say? The time for lectures about Gabe's worthiness is past!"

Jane nodded and heaved a sigh. "You have a point there, Harper."

"Does she?" Mike retorted.

"Zoey is four right now," Jane replied. "What happens if she finds out about her father when she's fourteen? She'd be angry, confused, betrayed. She could run away! At least if Zoey meets her father now—even if he's not terribly reliable—it won't be a shock later on. We can help her deal with the reality of her father as she grows. It's better than dumping it on her all at once. Zoey is a lot like her mom."

Mike nodded slowly and turned toward Harper again. "Fine. So when is he set to meet her?"

"Tomorrow evening," Harper replied. "At my place. We'll have dinner, and…I suppose I'll make the introductions."

Jane and Mike exchanged a long look. Harper had disappointed them, and she hated that. They'd been in this together from the start. And when Harper found out that she had custody of her goddaughter, she'd relied on the Murphys' reassurance that she was the right choice. Tonight, she'd let them down.

"You know how much I love Zoey," Harper said earnestly. "I'm going to protect her. You *know* that."

"There are some things you can't protect your child from," Jane said, her chin quivering. "We learned that the hard way."

Was Gabe Banks one of those disasters? Harper sent up a prayer of wordless panic. She could only trust that honesty was still the best policy, even when it came to a precious little girl she could no longer live without.

"Andrea knew where to come when she needed support," Mike said gruffly. "And so do you. I know your dad isn't feeling too well lately, so if you need help dealing with Gabe, you come tell me. I'll set him straight."

Harper smiled mistily. "Thanks, Mike."

Mike Murphy was a dad through and through, and the death of his daughter hadn't changed that protective instinct inside of him. He was a stalwart grandfather and like a second dad to Harper half the time. She'd keep his offer in mind.

"I'd better get Zoey home," Harper said, glancing at her watch.

"When will you tell her about her father?" Jane asked softly.

"Before Gabe arrives," Harper replied. "That way she can understand who he is."

Jane leaned over and gave Harper a squeeze. "You call Mike if you need him."

Harper chuckled. "I've got Gabe in hand. No worries there."

And she wished she felt as confident as she sounded. Harper went into the living room and scooped the little girl up into her arms. Zoey woke up enough to get into a more comfortable position before her eyes drooped shut again.

"Night-night, sweetie," Jane said, pressing a kiss against the girl's forehead. Then Jane met Harper's gaze. "Be careful."

Harper didn't know how deep that warning ran, but she took it to heart. Gabe was a risk—both to their easy balance here in Comfort Creek, and to her own emotional stability if she allowed herself to soften to him too much. Because Harper always had understood why her friend had fallen for this bad boy so hard. Gabe was disarmingly charming, broken—and what woman didn't like the challenge of being a man's saving grace? But a woman couldn't do God's job in a man's heart—better women than her had tried it.

For Zoey's sake, Harper needed to keep her head on her shoulders.

That Sunday, Gabe almost attended church. He put on a pair of khaki pants and even went so far as to iron a button-down shirt, and then he stared at the iron for a good while, unplugged it, and put his clothes away again. He couldn't do it.

Gabe went to church every Sunday back in Fort Collins, but Fort Collins was different. That was the home he'd made for himself as a grown man, away from all the jagged memories that Comfort Creek held for him. But Hand of Comfort Christian Church simmered old resentments. The thought of walking back into that church made his teeth clench. They could remember his grandmother any way they liked—he knew the truth about her. But he was no longer a lost kid, acting out. He was now a grown man, a police officer and a father...that last one still felt surreal. But that didn't mean he had it in him to sit in that church, rehashing those helpless feelings.

When six o'clock came around, Gabe arrived at Harper's door dressed in those khakis and the freshly ironed button-down shirt. He held a pair of toy handcuffs in one hand—it seemed silly to wrap them—and stared down at his shoes while he waited for Harper to answer.

The door opened, revealing Harper dressed in a soft green sweater that brought out the sparkling green of her eyes. Her red hair hung in spiral curls, free around her shoulders, and she stepped back in a gesture of welcome.

"Hi," he said, and he glanced around to see Zoey standing next to the couch, eyeing him speculatively. She wasn't the same bouncing kid from earlier, so he could only guess that Harper had filled her in. He had the sudden urge to apologize.

"Thanks for coming," Harper said, a smile toying at her lips. "Very prompt."

Gabe glanced down at his watch, then shot her a bashful grin. "First impressions, and all."

For one little girl, at least. Harper put a hand on his arm, and the warmth of her touch calmed his heart just a little bit.

"Hi, Zoey," Gabe said.

"This is..." Harper looked up at him questioningly.

"She can just call me Gabe," he said quickly.

"This is Gabe," Harper said, crossing the room, and squatting down next to the little girl. "Remember how we talked about how every family is different? And how we all have a mom and a dad? Well, Gabe is a part of our family. He's your dad."

A part of their family. He'd never quite looked at it that way before, and he watched conflicting emotions battle across Zoey's little face.

"I don't want a dad," Zoey whispered, and Gabe's heart sank. Yeah, he didn't really blame her. She had some great women in her life, and Gabe wasn't exactly the dad any little girl dreamed of.

Harper looked over at him, and Gabe smiled past his feelings and shrugged. He had good practice with that—it was his go-to move.

"Well, Gabe has come for dinner," Harper said. "I

thought it would be nice if we could all get to know each other a little better."

"Is he gonna live with us?" Zoey asked hesitantly.

"No!" Harper laughed. "No, no, no... Every family looks different, sweetie. In some families, the mom and the dad aren't married. That's what our family is like. You and I live together, and Gabe—" She looked over at him again.

"I'm just here for dinner," he said with a reassuring smile. "And then I'll go away. So no worries."

It looked like Zoey was in a bit of hurry to get rid of him, and he glanced around awkwardly. Harper's home was small, but pleasantly furnished. The gray couch had different colored throw pillows—blue, pink, yellow—and on the wall over a fireplace hung a bright painting depicting a meadow of wildflowers. The space was fresh and clean—a cloth tub of toys in one corner betraying a recent cleanup. The scent of garlic and spaghetti sauce permeated the air.

"Have a seat," Harper said. "Dinner will be ready soon. Spaghetti is Zoey's favorite."

"Mmm." Gabe looked in the girl's direction again. "I like it, too."

Zoey was silent—no more offers of pictures from her, apparently. Harper headed toward the kitchen, and Gabe stared after her in a mild panic. She couldn't just leave him alone with the kid! He looked back over at Zoey.

"I'm a surprise, aren't I?" Gabe asked.

Zoey didn't say anything. Instead, she went to the cloth bin and pulled out a doll. She angled to the other side of the room and sat down on the floor with her doll, casting Gabe a sidelong look. He had no idea what he was supposed to do. This kid hadn't asked for a dad, and here he was, invading her space.

"Uh, Harper—" Gabe crossed the room and poked his head into the kitchen. Harper stood at the sink, pouring a pot of noodles into a colander.

"Hi," she said. "Everything okay?"

No, it wasn't. He looked over at Zoey, and she was regarding him in silent disapproval, and then back at Harper. "Just thought I'd offer a hand."

"Go talk to her," Harper said, lowering her voice. "Just…say hi."

"I tried that. She doesn't seem to like me much."

Harper nodded, her smile slipping. "Yeah, I know. It's hard for her. She's lost a lot, and maybe I should have given her more warning, I don't know…"

It wasn't Harper's fault, though. This wasn't going to be an easy introduction, regardless. He looked back toward the little girl, and he realized he'd never felt more insecure in his life. He could deal with criminals, drug addicts, beautiful women—but that little girl was scarier than all the others combined.

"Zoey!" Harper called. "Why don't you come help me? I need someone to get the juice from the fridge!"

Zoey slowly rose to her feet and ambled into the kitchen. She sidled past Gabe and leaned her little shoulder into Harper's leg. There, she deflated with a deep sigh. The poor kid. His heart went out to her. Harper leaned down and gave Zoey a squeeze. She murmured something in her ear, and Zoey looked back at Gabe.

"Go on," Harper said.

"Mommy says you want juice," Zoey said.

"Uh—" Gabe nodded. "Yes, please."

Zoey went to a bottom cupboard and pulled out a

juice box. "You can take that home with you," she said, handing it up to him.

He looked over Harper and he caught the laughter sparkling in her eyes.

"The jug in the fridge," Harper chuckled. "Zoey, you're a character today!"

"You don't like the idea of having a dad, do you?" Gabe asked as Zoey carried a sloshing jug of red juice to the table.

"I got a Mommy here and Mommy in heaven," Zoey said. "And two grandmas and two grandpas."

"I get it," he said. Then he remembered the toy handcuffs in his pocket. "I brought you something, though."

Zoey's gaze brightened somewhat, and she eyed him with more curiosity. Gabe pulled the plastic cuffs from his pocket.

"What's that?" Zoey asked, not moving.

"Handcuffs. I'm a police officer, remember? Well, I thought you might like your own handcuffs, so you can arrest your mom from time to time."

A smile tickled the corners of the girl's mouth, and she came closer to get a better look.

"For me?" she asked hopefully.

"For you," he said with a nod. "Look—" He gave her a quick lesson on how the latch worked. "And now you can arrest people."

Zoey slapped a cuff on Gabe's wrist. "Like that!"

"But you have to say, 'You're under arrest,'" Gabe said. "Or they don't know what's happening."

"You're under arrest!" Zoey said, and she tugged at the cuff, trying to get it off. Gabe released the latch and Zoey looked down at the cuffs in satisfaction. Maybe there was a little bit more of him in this kid, after all.

"The stores weren't open," he said, glancing over at Harper.

"It looks like you did just fine," she replied with a small smile.

Harper had the food on the table—a heaping dish of noodles next to a bowl of steaming sauce. Three plates were laid with three glass tumblers waiting for that plastic jug of juice. It reminded him of TV family dinners—the kind he'd see on sitcoms. It felt oddly intimate.

"Come, have a seat," Harper said. Zoey beelined to the chair with a yellow booster seat attached, and Harper gestured Gabe toward another chair.

Gabe was a big man, and the table seemed to be of more feminine proportions. He eased himself slowly onto a chair and scooted it up. When they were all seated, Harper bowed her head.

"Lord, thank You for the food before us, the family and friends beside us and…" Harper paused "…the love between us. Amen."

Yeah, well, maybe there wasn't a whole lot of love lost between himself and Harper, but he was glad to see that Zoey had such a loving home. It took some of the pressure off. She didn't need him.

They raised their heads and Harper put a pleasant smile on her face. "So, Gabe. Maybe you could tell Zoey a little bit about you."

"Oh." Gabe nodded. "Uh, I'm thirty-two years old. As we've established, I'm a police officer. I like using handcuffs a lot, and red juice is my favorite."

"I like purple juice," Zoey said solemnly.

"Purple is in my top three," Gabe said, meeting her gaze with equal solemnity.

Zoey nodded slowly, seeming to accept this. "Okay, then. I also like princess crowns."

"Yeah?" Gabe pretended to be surprised. "I can see the appeal there. All sparkly and stuff. Can't say I've ever worn one myself. How do you feel about tools? Because I like tools a lot."

A smile broke over Zoey's face. "Yeah, I like tools!"

He hadn't felt anything besides trepidation up until now, but looking at those gray eyes and the tiny cleft in her chin, his heart melted just a little. She didn't feel like his, exactly, but she might not hate him quite so much. That was something.

Tools. Tiaras. Purple juice.

Who was he kidding? He was in *way* over his head.

Chapter Six

After the meal, Harper cleared the table and Zoey put her plate on the counter—the job that was expected of her after dinner each night.

"Thanks, sweetie," Harper said, and she wondered if Zoey understood what was happening here tonight. Did the word *father* mean anything to her at this young age? She'd never had a dad before. Granted, she'd seen that other children had daddies, but she'd never asked about her own. Four years old didn't seem mature enough to grapple with those questions of parentage.

"Let me wipe the table off." Gabe's arm brushed against hers as he reached for the tap. He was warm, and smelled musky and just a little bit like cinnamon. Comforting—which was frustrating. She glanced up at him, noticing just how tall and broad he was up close, then dropped her gaze.

Gabe didn't look like a dad. He was roguishly handsome, had an air of confidence that bordered on flirtation. Gabe seemed like a perfectly responsible adult, but men grew into fatherhood—it changed them, tamed them. Gabe was far from tame.

"Thanks." It was a nice gesture, and her arm felt a little cold as he moved away, back to the table. It was his charm that was so frustrating. She'd never been completely immune to his good looks, but she'd known what she wanted—marriage, kids. She had standards and priorities, and she'd never been the kind of woman who took too many risks.

As well as that worked out, she thought wryly. She was thirty-two and still hadn't found her guy. She was ready for married life, but God hadn't sent her the right man.

"Zoey, while I wash up the pots, why don't you show Gabe your unicorn show on TV?" Harper suggested.

"Does he like unicorns?" Zoey asked skeptically, and Harper chuckled, reaching into the sink for the plug, but as she did, she felt a tug and a sharp sting.

"Ouch!" She pulled back without even thinking, and her finger came up bloody.

Harper clamped a hand over her finger and blood dripped onto the floor. She shut her eyes, willing the kitchen to stop spinning.

"Mommy's bleeding!" Zoey squeaked.

"I'm fine, Zoey," Harper said. Zoey hated blood, but it was normally the child with a skinned knee and not Harper bleeding onto the kitchen floor. Harper felt a warm hand clamp over her wrist and she opened her eyes to stare straight into a broad chest. She tipped her chin upward to find Gabe looking down at her.

"You look woozy," he said.

"It surprised me," she said, but she couldn't help feeling annoyed with herself. As a single mother, she didn't have the luxury of getting lightheaded at the sight of blood. She was the go-to for every emergency now, and she felt as if she still had to prove herself in that arena.

Gabe grabbed a dish towel. "You terribly attached to this?" he asked. "It's about to get bloody."

"It's fine." She smiled shakily, wishing that she'd pulled off the confidence she'd intended.

"Now open your hand." His grip was gentle but steely strong, and she didn't have much choice but to do as she was told. She let go of her finger as he lifted her hand for a quick inspection. Then he clamped the towel over her finger and gave her a boyish grin.

"You'll live," he said.

"Does it hurt, Mommy?" Zoey asked, eyes wide.

"A bit," Harper admitted.

"You need a Band-Aid," Zoey confirmed. Her daughter's panic seemed to be subsiding, and curiosity was taking over. "Maybe two. Or three. You never know."

"She does," Gabe confirmed. "Do you know where they are?"

"In the bathroom," Zoey replied.

"Can you get some?" he asked.

Zoey nodded sagely, then turned and dashed out of the kitchen. Gabe loosened his grip on Harper's finger to take another look. She watched his face for a reaction, and got nothing. He must see a whole lot worse than a cut finger when he was on the job.

"Do you want stitches?" he asked.

"Is it bad enough?" she asked with a wince.

"I don't know… I'm on the fence about it. Up to you. I can bandage you up real good, or I can take you to the hospital."

"No, no." Harper shook her head. She realized belatedly that he'd entirely taken control of the situation, and she wasn't sure how she felt about that. This was her home—he was just visiting, and her sense of control was starting to seep away. This wasn't the plan. "I can bandage myself, you know," she said.

"Yeah? And hold pressure on it at the same time?" Gabe looked down at her, flinty eyes pinned to hers, and she felt her heart flutter in her chest. What was it with this man? But this was no different than him turning the high beams on Officer Tammy in the police station break room, and Harper was the one woman who wouldn't melt for him. Not visibly, at least.

"Fine. I'll accept the help," she said, but it sounded irritable even in her own ears.

Zoey came back into the kitchen with a box of princess Band-Aids, and Gabe nodded toward the kitchen table.

"Go sit," he said, and when Harper shot him an annoyed look, he added, "Please."

Harper did as she was told, and Gabe settled in a chair opposite her and set to work. His hands were warm and confident.

"You don't like it when I get bossy," he said conversationally as he worked.

"You know anyone who does?" she retorted.

A smile flickered at the corners of his lips. "It might have a tiny bit to do with why I'm here to begin with."

"Well, why?" Zoey asked, suddenly interested.

Harper and Gabe both looked over to Zoey and were silent for a beat. Then they both answered, "Nothing."

Harper laughed. "Sweetie, it's just grown-up stuff. Why don't you get the unicorn show started?"

Zoey didn't need to be asked twice, and she bounced from the room. Gabe finished bandaging Harper's finger and released her hand. It was well done, and she smiled. It felt comforting to have another adult to be sharing moments like these—grown-up "secrets."

"I don't know how much of this she understands," Harper admitted.

"She knew she didn't want a dad—that's something." His smile was an eyelash shy of humored.

"You don't have to want a father to have one," Harper said, returning his smile faintly. "Or a daughter, for that matter."

Gabe's gaze moved in the direction of the living room. "I don't want her to grow up knowing that I hadn't wanted—" He didn't finish. "It's…cruel."

"I'd never tell her that," Harper said.

"Other people around here?"

"Your actions will speak louder than people's comments," she replied, and she wished that her words were a vote of confidence, but they weren't. She would just have to wait and see what happened with Gabe, and she'd do her best to fill in the gaps. She was already mentally preparing explanations for her daughter. *Your dad had limitations, sweetie. He couldn't be the father you needed, and he wanted what was best for you. That's why he left you with us in Comfort Creek…*

"She looks a lot like you," Harper said, and she felt a small stab of anxiety as she said it. It would be easier if Zoey looked nothing like her dad, if she'd taken after her mother a little more strongly. Gabe might be easier to file away when he eventually left town, but having looked at Zoey and Gabe from across the table, she'd been struck by their similarities—from the clefts in their chins to the way they held their forks. Father and daughter were awfully alike.

"Poor kid," Gabe said, and she could tell he was trying to joke, but he didn't quite pull it off.

"If I'd known about Zoey, I would have—" Gabe stopped. "I don't know. I'd have done the right thing."

"You mean, you'd have gotten married?" she asked, mildly surprised. It was a sad thought to think that Andrea might have missed her chance at a requited love if she'd only told Gabe about her pregnancy instead of running away.

Gabe sighed. "Getting married isn't always the right choice, you know."

"Not when the parents have made a baby?" Harper asked.

"Oh, come on, Harper! Parents who are married for the sake of the children end up messing the kids up in whole new ways. We've all seen it—it's hard to watch. Marriage is about something deeper and more profound than that."

She eyed him skeptically. "I thought you weren't the marriage and kids kind of guy."

"I'm not, but that isn't because I don't respect the institution. I don't think two people should be getting married without an earth-shaking kind of love. What can I say? I'm an idealistic kind of guy."

But like she'd just told him, actions spoke louder than words, and so far she'd only seen Gabe run from relationships. The TV in the living room started to play a familiar theme song, and Harper shook her head. She wasn't going to make sense of this man, and it didn't matter. They were co-parents, not even exes! As long as he was a good father to Zoey, that was all that mattered.

"Zoey's waiting. Unicorns are very important. You should know that up front."

"All right." He sobered. "Lead the way."

* * *

Unicorns. Gabe repressed a sigh. His daughter—he was still adjusting to even thinking the word—was going to introduce him to a whole other world of little girl stuff, and he had to admit that he was scared. There was no time to adjust, to get used to the idea. Right now, he was running on instinct—be nice, smile, charm the kid. But that couldn't last, could it? Eventually, he'd be forced to parent in some capacity, and charm wasn't going to cut it.

Zoey was curled up on the floor with a giant pillow, and he sank into the couch next to Harper. She cast him a smile, and he felt a rush of uncertainty. What was he doing here? When he imagined what this meeting would be like, he'd thought there would be less…kid stuff. Was that naive of him?

"So…unicorns," Gabe said.

"It's a good show," Zoey said. "I watch it before bed sometimes when I can't sleep."

"Ah. So unicorns make you sleepy?" he asked.

"Unicorns are wonderful." Zoey eyed him with slight mistrust. "Really wonderful."

He wasn't sure how to answer that, and he looked over at Harper questioningly.

"All right, Zoey," Harper said with a chuckle. "I told you they were important."

The DVR recording began. It was about as agonizing as he expected it to be. He'd never been a big fan of children's television, but Zoey seemed to be enthralled by the story of a unicorn whose horn was too glittery. At least, he'd assumed she was enthralled until he heard soft snores coming from the direction of that giant pillow.

"She must have been tired," Harper whispered.

"Yeah, looks like."

Zoey looked smaller now that she was sleeping all curled up on that pillow. She looked more fragile, more in need of protection. She was this rambunctious, tender little responsibility that had been thrust onto him… and he had no choice. Whether it was good for the kid or not, she was his.

"Thanks for having me over." Gabe kept his voice low. "I appreciate getting to meet her…properly."

Harper nodded. "Thanks for coming."

So formal, and yet Harper still made him feel things he didn't want to feel. She'd always had that effect on him. She looked paler in the low light, her eyes luminous behind those tortoiseshell glasses. Gabe tore his gaze away from hers and pushed himself to his feet.

"So what do we—" He stopped when Zoey shifted in her sleep, nearly waking. That wasn't the plan. He glanced toward the door and Harper pointed and nodded. They'd step outside. It was probably better that way. The TV show droned on, and Gabe slipped on his jacket and shoes as Harper did the same, except she wore a pair of slippers and pulled on a bulky sweater.

The evening was chilly, and he led the way outside and into the yard. It was dark already, and the moon had risen in a milky orb, large and bright. The grass was starting to get a lace of frost around the fence posts, and the chill air smelled like leaves, dew and sunsets.

He met Harper's gaze.

"So…where does this leave us?" he asked. "What do you need from me?"

"I don't actually know." Her cheeks flushed pink. "You'd think I'd have figured that out, huh?"

"I was hoping so." He smiled wanly. "I have no idea

how to be a dad. My grandmother made everything about appearances—making sure that she didn't look bad. I just have a feeling that my first instincts here are going to be wrong."

"You looked like you were fine tonight," Harper said with a faint shrug.

She hadn't seen it—she'd never seen *him*. She'd looked right past him, never seen his very human heart. Tonight, he was far from "fine" with his daughter. But that was the way it had always been with Harper, even back when they were teens. He'd been head over heels for her, and she'd brushed him off like an afterthought.

"Well, I guess I fake it well. I always did."

"You mean when we were kids," she said. "I wish I'd noticed some warning signs or something."

"Think about it—I was angry, I was dating way too young, looking for love in all the wrong places... That wasn't normal behavior."

"I guess. I mean, you didn't seem like you were being abused." She met his gaze, sympathy mingling with guilt in those green eyes.

"Yeah, well, no one else noticed, either. My grandmother was a pro when it came to preserving appearances, so don't feel too bad."

Her eyes pooled with sadness, and Gabe reached out and moved a curl away from her forehead. She dropped her gaze as his fingers touched her silky skin, and he pulled his hand back. Why had he done that? There was just something about the honesty in her eyes... "I might not be family-man material, but I've got some good reasons for that, at least. You remember when I used to try to get you to go out with me?" he asked with a small smile.

"Vaguely." She looked away. Embarrassed? She

shouldn't be the one to feel stupid for that. "You asked out every girl."

"I asked them out, I flirted, and I played around," he agreed. "I only asked you out once, though, and I never played games with you."

"That's supposed to tell me something?" Harper dropped her hands. "I was just another girl you flirted with!"

"No, you weren't." His voice lowered to a rumble. "You were the one girl I really liked. I didn't fool around like I did with the other girls because when you shot me down, it actually hurt."

"Me?" She still seemed to not quite believe him. "I was quiet, bookish, kind of nerdy... You dated the cool girls."

"They'd have me." A smile twitched up one side of his mouth. "And you weren't nerdy, you were mysterious. A thinker...beautiful."

"Oh..." Harper pushed her hair away from her face, and she looked bashful again. He'd embarrassed her. She didn't seem used to compliments. She'd never softened to his charm, not even back then. But he was being completely honest. Harper had taken his breath away, and he sincerely wished that he'd stopped reacting to her like this over the years, but if anything, she was a slow burn—getting deeper and more beautiful as the years passed. She *still* took his breath away.

"Anyway," he said, clearing his throat. "I'll be working out my issues for a long time to come. But I'm honest, I work hard, and I'm a stubborn lout when it comes to criminals. I'm one of those guys who doesn't stop. It's hard to beat a guy who won't quit. I'm no prize boyfriendwise, but I'm a good cop. So whoever robbed your store just messed with the wrong man."

"I should be grateful for that," Harper said.

"Yeah. I'm good for something." He smiled ruefully. "I'm a better guy to have on your side than you think, Harper."

The wind picked up and Harper hunched her shoulders against the chill. They stepped toward each other as if on instinct—bracing against the damp, autumn cold. They ended up closer together than either seemed to expect, because Harper's eyes widened in surprise, just as another curl tumbled in front of them. Gabe reached to move it away from her face, and as he did, his gaze caught hers. Her lips parted as if she meant to say something, and he was struck anew by her untarnished beauty. Faint freckles were sprinkled across her nose, her milky skin glowing in the moonlight. Her lashes—dark auburn—brushed her cheeks when she blinked, and his breath caught. He wanted to pull her into his arms, be a human shield from both bad guys and the cold... He wanted to close those last inches between them, dip his head down and capture those soft, pink lips with his—and he caught himself leaning down.

What was he thinking? He knew better than to let his mind go down the garden path like that.

"I, uh—" Gabe cleared his throat, and closing his eyes for a moment, he tried to banish the image of a kiss he longed for. "I'd better get going. It's late."

"Me, too." Harper's response sounded breathy, and she took a step back. "I have to get Zoey into bed."

She met his gaze once more, then turned away. Gabe watched as Harper walked briskly back toward the front door, her sweater held close around her shoulders. She turned before she opened the door, and she seemed to have her reserve back. She met his gaze with an unreadable expression, and then disappeared inside. The door shut with a soft click, and he was left alone in the yard.

"Not the plan…" he muttered to himself as he headed for his vehicle.

That hadn't been the plan at all. He knew what he could offer, and he'd been praying for God to help him heal from all of it—including whatever residual feelings he'd been carrying around for Harper all these years.

Lord, keep me professional, he prayed in his heart. *I can't keep making the same mistake…*

He knew what he could offer. So why did he keep falling for women who wanted the very thing he couldn't provide? He was a cop, a protector, a stubborn lout who never quit. But he was not, and never would be, a family man.

And yet he'd have to figure out fatherhood somehow… He wanted to pray about that, and he didn't know how.

Chapter Seven

Harper closed the door behind her, then leaned against it with a shaky sigh. What had just happened out there? Gabe Banks was heartbreak waiting to happen, but she'd never looked up at *any* man and felt her heart flutter and her stomach float. He was different out there tonight—strong, muscular, vulnerably open... Still, she knew better! So why had she found herself breathless, looking up into those intense eyes and wondering if he was about to kiss her?

More to the point—would she have stopped him?

"Yes!" she said out loud, and Zoey stirred in front of the TV. Harper sighed and rubbed her hands over her face. Yes, she'd have stopped him, but it would have taken a great deal of self-control to do so. This was exactly the thing she'd been warning Andrea about. A man could lure a woman in, but that didn't mean he had anything at all to offer for the long term. And Harper wasn't a woman who wanted to be conquered or worn down. She wanted a man who made sense on a head level as well as a heart level.

Harper went to the window just as Gabe's truck

pulled out of the driveway. She leaned her forehead against the chilly glass and heaved a sigh. The problem with Gabe was that he wasn't quite so easy to dismiss. He was a wounded guy who was dealing with childhood abuse and some really hard memories. He was deeper than Harper liked to admit.

But that didn't make him kissable. Or dateable. It certainly didn't make him marriageable. It just made him harder to brush off.

Harper used the remote to turn the TV off, then bent down next to her daughter. *Their* daughter—in the least traditional of ways. She smoothed a hand over Zoey's forehead.

"Sweetie," she murmured. "Time for bed…"

Zoey blinked blearily up at Harper, and she gathered the girl in her arms. Zoey still fit into her arms nicely, and Harper ambled down the hallway toward Zoey's bedroom. This choice to tell Gabe about Zoey had eased her conscience, but it was also going to complicate her life. Not only did she have to learn how to parent, she'd have to learn how to co-parent with a man who'd just confessed to having had some very real feelings for her back when she thought he was just passing the time with some flirting.

Nothing about this was going to be simple, was it?

The next morning, Harper poured Zoey her breakfast cereal while she munched on some buttered toast of her own.

"So what did you think of your dad?" Harper asked.

"I don't know," Zoey said thoughtfully.

"Does he seem nice?" Harper asked.

"I liked the bracelets," she said, holding up the toy handcuffs.

Harper chuckled. "They're very nice. And they're called handcuffs, sweetie."

"I call them bracelets."

"Okay. No arresting the other kids today in pre-school."

"Aw!" Zoey's face fell, and Harper laughed softly.

"Your teacher will take the handcuffs away if you do."

"Fine," the girl sighed. "No arresting my friends…"

Harper didn't know what she was expecting from her daughter. Zoey was too young to grasp the import of having met her dad. At four, she still expected the world to revolve around her. But those handcuffs—they'd been a more enlightening gift than Gabe probably realized. Harper had never spotted it before, but Zoey just might have her dad's penchant for law enforcement.

After Harper dropped Zoey off at preschool, she headed over to Blessings Bridal to meet the glass company that was replacing the broken front window. She unlocked the front door and let herself in. She was ready to reopen again—any extra days closed were bad for the bottom line. As she turned toward the back room, there was a tap on the front door. She spotted Gabe in the door window, dressed in his plainclothes.

Harper forced what she hoped was a natural-looking smile to her face and walked over to unlock the door for him.

"Hi," he said as she pushed the door open.

"Hi." She swallowed, giving him a nod. "How are you?"

"Good…good…" He smiled tentatively. "Could I come in? I think I need to apologize for last night."

"Sure." What was she supposed to say? He was assigned to her shop for her protection, and if things got awkward between them, she couldn't exactly avoid the man. "But there are no apologies necessary."

What Harper really meant to say was that talking about that intense moment they'd shared last night was incredibly uncomfortable, and if she could avoid it, she would.

"No?" He eyed her uncertainly. "Look, that was…" He let out a pent-up breath. "I'm not hitting on you."

"Great." She wasn't sure if that was an improvement.

"That doesn't clear it up," Gabe said with a small smile. "What I mean is, yes, I find you attractive. More than attractive—gorgeous. I always have. You're a beautiful woman with a spark that I admire, but…whatever. That's no excuse."

Harper licked her lips. "But it wasn't only you."

"It wasn't?" He raised his eyebrows. "You sure about that?"

"I felt it, too," she admitted, her cheeks heating. "But obviously, we can't go there."

"Obviously," Gabe agreed, but his reaction was a little too quick to not bruise her ego just a little bit. "You're my daughter's mother, and I respect that. She needs you—and you and I have to maintain a good relationship for her sake. We can't just try this on for size and change our minds later without it affecting Zoey."

"That's a blessing, in a way. We don't have some failed romance between us. We're better for it."

"And we need to keep it that way," Gabe said. "I know that, and I won't…let things get complicated. If that makes you feel any better."

So they were on the same page—all very good. But

it didn't exactly fix whatever attraction was stewing between them. Maybe time would do the trick.

"Do you think you upset me?" she asked, only halfway teasing.

"Did I?" he countered.

She shrugged. "I'm a grown woman, Gabe. You aren't the first handsome man to have made eyes at me."

"Handsome?" There was a flirtatious dip in his voice and she cast him an exasperated look. "Sorry. Not that it matters."

Harper shook her head and suppressed a smile. "Attraction doesn't make a relationship functional, Gabe."

"Don't I know it." He cleared his throat. "How was Zoey? I mean, after meeting me, and all?"

Harper thought back on her morning. "I don't think she really understands it, truthfully."

"Maybe that's a good thing," he replied. "She has no expectations."

"But she will develop a few expectations as she gets older," Harper countered.

"Yeah, but right now, it might make us getting to know each other a little easier."

Harper nodded. She had to agree. "Whatever you do, please don't make any promises you can't keep."

"Like what?" he asked.

"I don't know. It's just—Zoey's been through so much this last year in losing her mom, coming to live with me, all the adjustment and grieving…" Harper sighed. "I don't know how much more disappointment she can take. So just…be careful."

"Okay." His gaze warmed as he met hers, and Harper broke the eye contact with a pang of guilt. God had brought Gabe into her path for Zoey's sake—she was sure of it. She wasn't going to conflate her own feelings of attraction with God's will.

There was another tap on the front door, and Harper looked over to see the man from the glass company. He wore a green uniform and gave her a cordial nod when he saw that he'd been noticed.

"He's here to fix the window," Harper said, glad for the interruption.

"Yeah?" Gabe frowned, and she could see the cop in him coming back to the surface. He was reserved again, granite. "Let me check his ID and I'll call the company, just to make sure."

That's why Gabe was here—protection. And just because feeling protected felt a whole lot like being loved, there was no reason to get the two confused. There would be no more moonlight moments like last night if she could help it.

"What's your name?" Gabe asked as he unlocked the front door. The man took one look at Gabe and took an involuntary step back. Gabe was used to that reaction. He was a big man, and if he didn't tone down his naturally brusque manner, he tended to intimidate. This morning, he didn't much care, though. He'd used up all his gentleness and consideration on the woman he was trying to protect.

"I'm Will Boyd from Glistening Glass. I was sent here for a window repair?" He glanced toward the boarded-up window, and another man in the same uniform came up behind him.

"Could I see your ID, please?" Gabe knew he sounded like a cop, even out of uniform, but he wasn't about to let just any guy in a glass company uniform into the store, either. If the robbers were going to come back and scope the place out, this would be an excellent way. Distracted as he was by finding out he was a dad…and by whatever he was trying not to feel for Harper…he was still here on a case.

The man fished out his wallet and showed his driver's license next to his work ID. William Franklyn Boyd. He'd do a quick background check, just to be on the safe side. The other man supplied his ID, too, and Gabe made a note of both names, then called the company. The men stood at the door looking mildly annoyed while Gabe confirmed them, and when he'd hung up again, he stepped back to let them in.

"Thanks," Gabe said, then looked over his shoulder at Harper when he heard her footsteps behind him. "I'll be back in a bit, okay?"

"Sure."

Now that they'd set things straight between them, it was best to get back to the reason he was here to begin with—catching whoever had robbed this place. He was better in this role, anyway. He knew how to check identities, how to trail crooks, gather evidence. He felt like he was actually doing something this way, not just wading through emotions. He'd never been good when it came to his deeper feelings because they were all tangled up with his abusive upbringing. And now, whatever attraction he was feeling for Harper was added to that mix.

Harper Kemp was off limits. Period. Whatever he felt with her in the moonlight didn't amount to anything in the daylight, and he'd best remember it. He wasn't a family man, and she was already a mother—to his daughter! Complicated, messy. It was great if they could be legitimate friends as they co-parented his daughter, but that was where it needed to stop.

William Boyd came inside the shop and Gabe eased past him and out onto the street. The brisk breeze felt good as he looked up and down that familiar old street. The road was dappled in shade from the golden leaves of overhanging branches. A warm dazzle of sunlight soaked into his shoulders.

Blessings Bridal was an old brick building, and with the boarded-over window it looked rather dismal. Sad. Faded. Like everything in this town, it seemed to him. Most people liked Comfort Creek. It was cute, they said. It had character. But this place felt more like a prison to him with the sordid stew of his childhood memories.

Gabe pulled the notebook from his pocket. He'd better make use of it if he wanted to continue to avoid book work in the basement.

Sycamore Drive, he wrote. *Memory: riding my bike with a bunch of other kids and dreading having to go home for dinner. I picked a fight with a smaller boy because I wanted somewhere to vent my frustration. I gave him a black eye and he went home crying. It didn't make me feel any better.*

Ricky Henson. That had been the kid's name. He'd been small and slender in build. Kind of gentle and bookish, but he enjoyed riding his bike like the rest of them. He'd been at the top of their class when they graduated high school, and he was a pharmacist in the city now, from what Gabe had heard, so he had grown up and made a success of himself.

Lord, what is the point of this? he silently prayed. *Let me catch whoever robbed Harper's store, and then get me back to the city where I can get away from these memories.*

He hadn't liked himself any more than his grandmother had liked him back then. What he'd hated most was that she'd been right. He'd been a rough kid—prone to fights, petty thefts and back talk. His anger had welled up and squeezed out in ways that even his grandmother hadn't known about. She only knew about the times he'd been caught.

And yet her dislike of him had stabbed deep. His own mother had dumped him on his grandmother's doorstep, and that abandonment had been a hard one to deal with, too. Then his grandmother would look at him with such disgust in her eyes, and he'd glower back at her as if he didn't care. But he had.

He snapped his notebook shut and put it back into his front pocket, and as he did so, a black BMW eased to a stop across the street from Blessings Bridal. It was a new model, and the metal shone like obsidian. Gabe watched the vehicle for a moment. BMWs didn't exactly blend into the surroundings here in Comfort Creek. The driver didn't seem to take much notice of Gabe, but he did settle his attention on the store. Not an idle glance—a direct stare—and the hair on Gabe's neck stood on end. He reached back to touch his gun in the holster under his shirt and turned his steps in the direction of the car.

Gabe ambled across the road and then approached the vehicle from behind, being careful to stay in the driver's blind spot.

"Hey, there," he barked, and he moved into view. The driver—a young, clean-cut, blond-haired fellow—stared at him surprise. "License and registration, please."

"Who are you?" the man demanded.

Gabe pulled out his badge. "The police. License and registration. Now."

"Uh—yeah, sure… Did I do something?"

The man supplied the required ID, and as Gabe looked it over, he raised an eyebrow. "Chris Holmes?"

"Yeah, that's me."

"I wouldn't have recognized you," Gabe said. "We were in the same graduating class. Gabe Banks."

"No way." Chris nodded slowly. "Long time. How are you doing?"

"Can't complain. I hear you're working the family business."

"That was always the plan," Chris said with a nod. "I'm looking for Heidi Kemp, actually. We're engaged—there's some news for you. Is she in there?"

"I was just in the store, and no. She's not around, right now."

Chris looked at his watch, then heaved a sigh. "Okay. So she lied."

"What are you talking about?" Gabe glanced over toward the store. He could see Harper through the unbroken side of the window, her glasses held in one hand, the end in her mouth. Her attention was on something he couldn't see.

"I've been trying to get Heidi to have breakfast with me for a week," Chris replied. "This morning's excuse was that she was doing a dress fitting at the store with her sister. I came by to surprise her with some cheese Danishes…but…yeah."

"You didn't go knock," Gabe said, sifting through this story for a hint of a lie. "So you obviously suspected something."

"I'm not supposed to see the dress." Chris shot him a bitter smile. "I was waiting for her to come out." He heaved a sigh. "Whatever. She's not here. I'll talk to her later."

The dress, and all that wedding stuff. Of course. Gabe looked past Chris to the paper bag beside him. "So…you gonna eat those?"

Chris eyed him uncertainly. "No. Go ahead." He passed him the bag, and Gabe opened it, snagging a glaze-crusted Danish from its depths.

"So what's up with Heidi?" Gabe asked, taking a bite and tucking it into his cheek.

"Honestly, man, I'm not sure what's going on."

"So this isn't the only time she's disappeared on you?" Gabe asked.

"She's just getting…distanced. I don't know. I think she might be getting cold feet."

"Women do that?" Gabe asked with a chuckle, but when he met Chris's miserable look, he sobered. "Look, from what I know, she and Harper are fighting over some dress."

"It's their grandmother's. An heirloom." Chris provided.

"Yeah, that's the one. So if they're altering an heirloom dress, I figure you're pretty safe."

Chris nodded a couple of times, then brightened. "That's a good point. I'm worried for nothing, aren't I?"

"For sure." Gabe shrugged. "Women are complicated. They confuse us at the best of times."

"No, you're right. I'll text her later. I've got a meeting in a few minutes anyway. If you see her, tell her I came by."

"Will do."

Chris leaned forward to start the car. He raised his hand in a farewell as he pulled away from the curb. That could count as a good deed for the day, but Gabe still wondered what Heidi was up to. She was definitely not in the store…

Whatever. As long as she wasn't cavorting with criminals, this wasn't his business. He picked up his cell phone and dialed the station. He had an ID to check for this William Franklyn Boyd. Due diligence. It was the one virtue his grandmother had taught him in all those years in hiding his life from her. Dot your *i*'s. Cross your *t*'s. Because he never knew who was watching.

He scanned the street once more, but there was no one else around. Someone *was* watching. He could feel it like a tingle on the back of his neck. These robbers would return. That was a guarantee. The only question was when.

Chapter Eight

Harper watched from across the store as the window repair men got to work removing shards of broken glass and peeling away the rubber seal. It would feel good to have the glass replaced. She wanted to reopen as quickly as possible, and yet she still didn't feel entirely safe.

"We're just going out to get the pane of glass," one of the workers said as the store phone rang.

Harper nodded in the men's direction. "Sure. No problem." She picked up the receiver. "Blessings Bridal, this is Harper speaking."

"Hi, Harper, I was hoping to catch you. This is Reverend Blake."

Harper had just seen the reverend on Sunday, and she smiled at the sound of his voice. "It's nice to hear from you, Reverend. What can I do for you?"

"You mentioned that Gabriel Banks is patrolling your shop," he said. "And I actually was hoping to get into contact with him. Is he there?"

"No, he's just popped out," Harper replied. "He'll be back, though. Should I get him to call you?"

"If he wants to, but it's simple enough. When his

grandmother passed away, there were a few personal items that I thought he might like to have."

"Oh…" Harper grimaced.

"I was only hoping you could pass along the message. I have the things here at the church office."

"I'll definitely let him know."

"We're praying for you, Harper," the reverend said. "I'm sorry about that robbery, and I'm personally praying for your continued protection."

"Thanks, Reverend. I appreciate that more than you know."

After she'd hung up, Harper breathed a sigh. What she needed was to reopen this store and get back into a rhythm. They not only needed the income, but she also needed the routine. This store wasn't just a job, it was her life, her history, and those criminals couldn't be allowed to take that away. She needed God's protection, and her life back.

The workers returned carrying a sheet of glass between them using rubber suction cup handles. Harper watched them for a moment, and glanced up as Gabe moved past them and pulled open the front door.

"It's coming along," Harper said with a smile. "Look at all that natural daylight."

The things one took for granted until the main window was boarded up. Gabe sauntered inside and stopped next to her, glancing back to the working men.

"Where's Heidi?" he asked, turning back toward her, and she eyed him in surprise.

"I don't know. Why?"

"Chris was looking for her."

"He should call her cell phone." She shook her head. "What's going on?"

"Probably nothing," Gabe replied. "But she's using dress fittings with you to put off her fiancé."

"What?" Harper brushed a curl out of her eyes. "Maybe he misunderstood."

"Yeah, sure." He didn't look entirely convinced, and Harper felt her irritation rise. She wasn't even sure why.

"I'm not responsible for my sister, you know. She's a grown woman!" Harper said a little more sharply than intended. Gabe didn't answer, but he did raise his eyebrows at her and she shook her head. "Look, you remember Heidi. She was always...flighty. But Chris is a great guy. We all love him, and she's excited to settle down. Maybe Chris is just getting prewedding jitters, seeing problems where there aren't any."

"I'm just passing along the message, Harper." His voice was a low rumble. "This isn't really my business."

No, it wasn't. Neither was it Harper's, really, but she did feel a sort of responsibility toward her sister. Heidi could be impetuous and she could live to regret that some days.

"Speaking of passing along the message," Harper said, "Reverend Blake called and said he has a few items that used to belong to your grandmother that he thought you might want."

Gabe looked away, sending a blazing glare toward the two workers. One froze, eyeing Gabe uncertainly. She'd never seen this side of him before—the intense, angry man before her. He was large, bristling, and definitely daunting. Not that she was afraid of him—not Gabe. She knew him too well for that. But he was making the workers nervous.

"Stop scaring the glass guys," Harper murmured.

"Sorry." His gaze whipped back toward her. "I hate this."

"I know." She winced. "The reverend doesn't know how complicated this is for you. He's like everyone else."

She wasn't sure if that was reassuring or not. Comfort Creek had let him down when he'd needed protection the most. And now he was back—offering the protection that he'd never gotten. The thought made a lump rise in her throat. They owed him…something.

"Old Reverend Blake was one of my grandmother's biggest fans," Gabe replied bitterly.

"He doesn't know what she did, Gabe." And if the reverend had known, he'd have intervened. Harper knew that for a fact. He'd called Social Services on another family not five years ago when he suspected child neglect. "Anyway, he just called."

"What items does he have?" Gabe asked.

"I don't know. He didn't say."

Gabe shoved his hands into his pockets and chewed on the side of his cheek. "Do you know what it's like to be running away from part of yourself?"

"No. Not really," she admitted, her voice barely above a whisper.

"It keeps circling back on you. Like a dog chasing its own tail."

She could see the emotion reflected in his eyes, but the rest of his expression was like granite. He seemed to hide an awful lot behind that chiseled mask of his. And maybe it was more than that—the deflective good looks, the charm, the flirting. At least the women didn't bother looking deeper. Harper never had.

"Do you want to see what it is?" she asked softly. "Maybe it will provide some closure."

"You think?"

She couldn't tell if that was sarcasm or not, but she plunged on. "My aunt and her sister fought like cats and dogs their whole lives, and when the oldest aunt passed away, the younger one was left with a lot of resentment and anger. But she ended up taking a teacup in memory of her sister—mostly because my mother foisted it upon her—and now, five years later, she drinks out of that teacup all the time. It gives her comfort."

"So what made it easier for your aunt?" he asked, crossing his arms over his chest. "It couldn't have just been the cup."

"Time, I suppose," Harper guessed. "I did ask her about it once. She said that her sister was in heaven, and she trusted Jesus to do some explaining on her behalf. With a little Heavenly perspective, her sister would be able to see that she wasn't so bad, after all. That was the way she saw it, at least."

"Huh." Gabe sighed resignedly. "You're the only one who knows about all of this, you know. Is that weird?"

"Maybe." She smiled, but then sobered. "But… I'm honored. And I do understand why it's so hard for you."

"Yeah?" The confidence slipped, and she saw uncertainty etched in his features just for a moment before it disappeared. "Maybe I'll be glad I picked it up. Maybe I won't. But I won't know unless I do it, right?"

"Do you want…company?" Harper asked cautiously. "Once the window guys are done, I could go with you to the church."

"I'm supposed to be tougher than this."

"No, you aren't," she replied with a shrug. "Believe it or not, Gabe, you're human."

He smiled ruefully. "If you're offering the company, I'll take it."

"Good. There should be just enough time before I pick up Zoey from preschool."

Harper looked out the new pane of glass, past the men who were sealing it into place, and she saw a patrol car easing by on the street.

Comfort Creek—the best patrolled town in America. It was supposed to be safe, but for some of them, it wasn't. There were bad guys with plans to come back to Blessings Bridal and finish the destruction they'd started, and there were people born and raised in this idyllic little town who hid wicked secrets underneath their glossy exteriors.

In a town that was supposed to be the safest community in the country, they still had to take care of each other.

Gabe had checked further into the glass company employees, and they were legitimate. No criminal records, good work histories. It was both a relief and an annoyance. A red flag with one of these guys would have at least given him a lead to work with. As it was, he was just waiting for the worst to happen, and Gabe didn't like that feeling of being out of control, especially when Harper and Zoey's safety were at risk. He'd only known about his daughter for a couple of days, but her presence in his world was already changing things…changing *him*. He'd do whatever it took to protect Harper, but with Zoey, his protective instinct sharpened.

Zoey was…his. Strange as that felt. And even if he'd

never make much of a dad, he made a fine cop, and right now, that's what both Harper and Zoey needed—police protection.

The men finished their work, leaving behind a gleaming new window. Harper stood for a minute or two, looking it over in satisfaction while Gabe watched her. Her frame was slim, and her red curls blazed in the afternoon sunlight. Stunning... Some women peaked in their younger years, while others just got more deeply beautiful as the years ticked by, and Harper seemed to be in the latter category.

"I feel better—it's back to normal in here," Harper said, turning toward him. "If they come back and break this, I'm going to scream."

"This one is personal for me, Harper."

"Because of Zoey," Harper concluded, and while she was partially right, it wasn't only Zoey that he'd been thinking of. Harper factored in, too. She'd called them a family before, and as his daughter's adoptive mother, she belonged to him in a way, too. He'd heard this kind of odd but meaningful connection described as *family* before, and it fit. There was nothing traditional about them, but that didn't change the fact that he was going to take care of the two of them. And he wasn't willing to admit any of it.

"I'm cooped up in Comfort Creek, and that puts me in a phenomenally bad mood. I'd rather put my time here to good use and catch these idiots," he said.

Harper smiled, then shrugged faintly. "I've been holding off on asking this because I didn't want to overstep, but...what did you say to your boss to get sent here?"

"I told my supervising officer exactly what I thought of him," he replied blandly.

"And you didn't have a glowing opinion of the guy, I take it."

"I thought he was petty, small-minded and had raised a spoiled brat of a son." Gabe raised his eyebrows. "Turns out it sounds even worse when you say it out loud."

Harper rolled her eyes, but he could tell she was suppressing laughter. "You're still the rebel, aren't you?"

"Rebel?" Gabe sighed. "I don't go against authority just for the sake of it anymore, but I'm less inclined to put up with garbage, and I've learned what I can change about myself and what I can't. So not a rebel, exactly. Just less optimistic."

Harper's expression turned sad and she met his gaze for a moment. "You're a Christian now, though. So optimism…isn't that just faith that God is still working things out for your good?"

"I'm a cop. I see the hard stuff, Harper. I know what people are capable of. It isn't a lack of faith, believe me. Maybe I just think that people are worse off than most people realize." He shot her a rueful smile. "My problem is that sometimes I say it out loud."

Harper glanced at her watch. "Are you ready to go see the reverend?"

"Sure. Let's get going. I'll drive. I'll bring you back here when we're done so you can get Zoey."

Nothing had changed in Comfort Creek in the years he'd been gone. Except for the death of his grandmother. The streets were the same; the easy rhythms of the community that made time seem to crawl by were the same, too. As was the way it felt to be in close proximity to

Harper Kemp. She'd always had this effect on him—
an instinct to try to prove something to her, to impress
her somehow. But who was he fooling? She knew too
much about him to be impressed.

The Hand of Comfort Christian Church was located
on Main Street, and Gabe eased into the parking lot,
his heart constricting the closer he got to the building.
He hated this place—he had for as long as he could remember. It represented his grandmother's polished ap-
pearance, so unlike her true nature at home. To him,
this church had been all preening and fakery.

Gabe parked in a spot next to the side door and
turned off the engine.

"You okay?" Harper asked.

"Why?" he grunted.

"You're glaring at the church wall like you might be
able to break it."

"Let's just get this over with."

He pushed open the driver's side door before she
could answer and stepped outside into the autumn chill.
Before, he'd wanted her company, but now he was re-
gretting that just a little. He kept forgetting how terrible he was at hiding his feelings, and he wasn't sure he
wanted an audience.

Too late, though. She got out of the car and when
she slammed the door behind her, they headed toward
the side entrance.

The door was unlocked, and Gabe held it open for
Harper to enter first. When he stepped inside the church,
it smelled just the same as it always had—slightly musty,
like old paper and disintegrating wood varnish. He knew

the way to the reverend's office, and he glanced into the church foyer on their way past.

So much the same, and yet so different. He wasn't a helpless kid anymore, and that definitely changed his perspective. He didn't feel trapped, but now he felt furious. He could see himself as a kid in that foyer, dressed in his Sunday best, standing next to his grandmother. He'd always done his best to be good, if only to escape punishment, but he'd mess up somehow. A forgotten handshake, an ill-timed joke. He'd never been good enough to escape Grandma's wrath. He'd only been a kid; someone should have stood up for him.

The reverend's office was at the end of the hall, and they could hear the soft murmur of voices as they approached. When they reached the door, which was propped open with a pile of hymnals, the church receptionist looked up with a smile.

"Hi, there," she crooned. "How can I help you today?"

"We're here to see Reverend Blake," Harper said. "Is he in?"

"He is." But this time, the voice belonged to the jovial reverend, and he came out from his office. He was a tall man with a large belly and a wide smile. He shook Harper's hand, then Gabe's.

"Long time, Gabriel," the reverend said, his smile slipping. "I'm so sorry about your grandmother's passing. She was a good woman. We all loved her here at Hand of Comfort. She put her heart and soul into this parish."

Gabe didn't trust himself to answer that. "Harper said you had something for me?"

"Yes, yes. Come into my office." Reverend Blake

led the way, and Gabe and Harper followed him into his office. The room wasn't large to begin with, and it was further dwarfed by the sheer size of the reverend. One wall was covered in books, and there were some pieces of ethnic art on the wall, most with inscriptions thanking the Hand of Comfort for mission trips.

The reverend let out a soft grunt as he lowered himself into his chair.

"On the other side of Jordan, I'll be as fit as you, Gabriel," the reverend said with a soft laugh. He opened a drawer and pulled out a box, sliding it across the desk toward Gabe. Gabe reached for the box, but didn't open it.

"Your grandmother wanted me to give you these items. She asked for it specifically." The reverend's gaze flickered toward Harper. "Maybe we could talk in private another time—"

"No, no, Harper's here for moral support, so you don't have to worry about her," Gabe said. He had no desire to do this without the buffer of another person in the room.

"As you know, Imogen was in the hospital for a couple of weeks before she passed away." Reverend Blake went on. "And she told me a great deal in that time. She had many regrets."

"Did she? I find that hard to believe."

The reverend winced. "She told me that she'd been too demanding in her expectations, and she wished that she'd been gentler. Your grandmother loved you deeply, and she only wanted the best for you."

Saving face to the end. Even on her deathbed, she clung to her side of that story—the loving grandmother who only wanted what was best for that useless child she'd been left with. But that wasn't the case at all. She'd wanted what was best for *her*—and Gabe had never fit that bill. Gabe felt his teeth grind, and his expression must have turned daunting because the reverend cast him a sympathetic look.

"Gabriel, what drove you away?" Reverend Blake asked quietly.

"Reverend, you don't need to worry about that," Gabe said, taking the box and tucking it under one arm. "Your duty is discharged. Thank you."

"She confessed that she was harsh with you," the older man went on. "And there was a lie she told you that she felt bad about later—"

"A lie?"

"She told you that the church paid for your camp trip that summer when you were twelve. It wasn't the church, son. It was money your grandmother had been saving up to replace that old car of hers. She thought the camp would do you good, and that it would matter more than the car would in the long run—"

"She paid for camp?" Gabe paused. "Why not tell me?"

"I don't know."

Grandma Banks hadn't been all bad. She'd baked a cake for him every birthday and let him choose the frosting. She'd buy him one of those candles in the shape of a number. She'd also insisted on him going to the barbershop once a month, and she'd put the money in his hand and tell him to leave the change as a tip. He'd always kept the change to spend later.

She'd been cold and proper, and angry as a viper when he messed up. But there had been a few tender memories mixed in, too, like the Christmas she'd bought him a leather jacket and he'd been over the moon because it was the one thing he'd really wanted. He'd found a twenty-dollar bill in one of the pockets.

Don't forget to tithe it was all she'd said. She'd wanted him to have some pocket money, too, apparently, and she'd stared at him pointedly until he dropped two singles into the offering plate the next Sunday.

She'd always made sure the fridge was full of food when he was a growing teen, which wouldn't have been cheap. He'd never gone without when it came to meals, and she'd made sure he wore decent clothes that fit. He'd assumed that was for appearances, though, because it had never come with a hug or a smile.

"I'm not defending her," the reverend went on. "The Lord will judge her now, not me. Or you."

"Reverend, she didn't love me," Gabe replied, his voice quiet. That wasn't anger; it was concession. Maybe she'd tried to and hadn't been able to summon it up. It was possible that not every child was lovable.

"I don't know if she did," the reverend replied. "I won't insult you by giving false assurances. All I know is what she told me in private—that she thought you were smart. She thought you'd make something of yourself. She felt responsible for how your mother turned out, but she saw better things for you. I didn't know about the abuse until she confessed it before her death, but she did tell me that her own mother had been terribly abusive toward her growing up, and she hadn't known any other way."

"Too little, too late," Gabe said with a shake of his head.

Harper's gaze whipped between them, but she didn't

say anything. Gabe turned for the door, and Harper followed him.

"Gabriel, she said something before she died…" the reverend said, his voice trembling.

Gabe froze, a deep sigh seeping out of him. Dying words. Did he want to hear this? But there was no walking away now. He turned back, licking his lips nervously.

"What did she say?" Gabe asked hollowly.

"She said, *Gabe, forgive me.* I thought she meant God—that she was asking God for forgiveness. But now… I think she meant you, son."

Forgiveness. After years of cold abuse and limited kindness, she'd wanted absolution on her death bed?

"Thanks, Reverend," Gabe said, and he turned for the door once more.

Harper said a few words of farewell, but Gabe didn't slow down. She caught up with him at the side door, breathing a little harder than usual.

"What?" he demanded, looking down into her upturned face.

"Nothing." She shrugged faintly. "Just making sure you're okay."

"Oh." He softened a little at that, and she opened the door for him this time. They went outside together, and Gabe looked down at the box in his hands.

"Are you going to open it?" Harper asked. "Or wait until you're alone?"

Gabe didn't actually want to wait until he was by himself. Having Harper here seemed to dissipate some of the power of those memories, so he pulled off the lid and looked inside. There were only two items: his grandmother's worn Bible and a Popsicle stick craft from his elementary school years in the shape of a house. He remembered making it, laboring over it longer than any of the other kids did, until the teacher had to tell him to stop.

He turned it over, and on the back was his childish print: *To Grandma. I love you.*

He'd *loved* his grandmother, and grief surged up inside of him like a tsunami, tears pricking his eyes and a lump closing off his throat. He'd loved her, and she'd pushed him aside. He'd loved her, and she'd withheld her own love in return unless he earned it…which he'd never done. He'd so stupidly loved that woman, and she'd only ever thrown his affection back into his face.

Why had she kept this little craft? He had no idea.

"Gabe?" Harper's expression was worried.

He swallowed hard. "It's nothing."

He could hear the ice in his voice, but when he looked over at her, her green gaze tugged at him. He closed his eyes. He didn't want that—to turn to her. He needed to find some steel inside of himself and carry on. Just like he'd always done.

Gabe felt her hand on his arm and he looked down at her. To be held… That's what he'd always wanted as a kid—just to have someone hold him, rock him. But as a teenager, he'd turned to girlfriends for that contact, and it had been all wrong. He wasn't going to make that mistake with Harper, either.

"I'm fine," he said, softening his tone. "It's—" He opened the box again. "It's Grandma's Bible and a craft I made as a kid. I guess she kept it. I have no idea why."

"She loved you," Harper said. "Maybe not very well, but she did."

Gabe looked down at the little Popsicle stick house

once more. "I worked so hard on this. I started over twice. I wanted it to be perfect." He sighed. "I was trying to be as good as possible to earn some basic affection, but I was never quite good enough. Neither was this stupid craft."

Harper didn't say anything, and he was grateful for that. He wasn't looking for any platitudes or religious affirmation. His relationship with God was raw and real—as far removed from the polished church experience he'd grown up with as possible. Gabe opened the back door of the SUV and tossed the box inside.

"Let's get going," he said.

His grandmother had wanted his forgiveness, but she did not have it. The minute his sensitivity training was done, he needed to get out of this town and put it behind him for good. The memories were too painful. His grandmother's grave, her memory, her last words— Comfort Creek could keep her.

Chapter Nine

The next day, Harper found Gabe distanced and introverted. She couldn't say that she blamed him, but he kept his distance, and while he was in and out of the store making his presence known, she felt his desire for space. That was probably for the best, anyway. She needed to keep her own emotions carefully sorted out, too.

That evening, after Zoey was in bed, Harper hung her grandmother's dress from a hook in the doorjamb between the kitchen and the living room. Harper fingered the aged lace—once white and now closer to ivory. It was perfect, though. There was no need to try to brighten the lace again, because it had the air of something intentionally antiqued. There were memories breathed into the fabric, history. Grandma and Grandpa Kemp had both passed away already, but theirs had been a long and steady love—the kind Harper longed to find for herself.

At thirty-two, Harper was starting to wonder if marriage would ever happen for her. Harper was the more serious older sister, and Heidi was the one who sparkled.

Her smile lit up a room, and her laugh could draw every male ear around. Heidi was cute and loveable. And she was getting married first.

Jealousy wasn't an attractive emotion, and while Harper tried to tamp it down, she had to admit to feeling just a little bit jealous of her sister. Everything came easily for Heidi. And she'd wear Grandma's dress first.

Lord, I'm happy for my sister. I am! But while You're blessing her, please don't forget me. I want this, too. But with the right man. I don't want to waste my time on someone You haven't sent my way.

The dress hung in the doorway, the light from the living room shining through the lace. Harper had marked the new hemline with a chip of soap and some pink-headed pins on both layers—the taffeta and the lace. She held the heavy metal shears in one hand, but she couldn't bring herself to make the cut. Slicing through that material—it felt almost violent.

But this was Heidi's wedding, and Harper had to remember that. This wasn't about her at all. It was her sister's big day. And yet, her mind wasn't completely fixed on her sister's wedding, either. Gabe's face kept popping into her mind. Truth be told, she'd been thinking of him all afternoon, ever since he'd dropped her off so she could pick up Zoey.

"Cut it out," she told herself aloud.

But this wasn't about his good looks, or the way her stomach had of flip-flopping at the least opportune times when he was looking down at her the way he did… This was about that tormented look on his face when he opened that box. What had his grandmother done to him to cut him that deeply? Imogen Banks had always struck Harper as so…proper.

But there was guilt mixed in there, too, because Harper had judged Gabe pretty harshly, as well. Mind you, he *wasn't* any good for Andrea—she had to stand by that. But she'd never even considered the pain under the surface for Gabe Banks, and she wished that she would have. She'd never seen such pain in a man's eyes before today. Why had no one stepped in?

Her cell phone rang, and Harper glanced at the number. It was her sister. She put the shears down on the table and hit the talk button.

"Hi, Heidi," she said.

"Hi! How are you?"

"Not bad." Harper attempted to cheer up her tone a little. Gabe had shared something personal with her, and she sensed the privacy of that moment they'd shared. She wouldn't share it with anyone else. He could count on her for that much. "I had a busy day. How about you?"

"I got together with Sadie about the seating charts, and guess what?" Sadie was one of Harper's close friends, and the wedding planner for Chris and Heidi's wedding.

"I don't know. I can't guess," Harper said, eyeing the hanging dress moodily, her gaze moving from pin to pin.

"She's pregnant."

"What?" Harper's stomach dropped. Yet another friend married and having a baby. "Sadie's not trying to get pregnant. She told me herself—she's focusing on her event planning business right now."

"I know what I saw," Heidi replied breezily. "She was drinking mint tea at the coffee shop, took one bite of a sandwich, and then threw up in the garbage can."

"There is such a thing as the flu," Harper replied with a sigh. "Don't start rumors."

"There's also such a thing as morning sickness," her sister quipped.

"If she is pregnant, I'm thrilled for her. But seriously, Heidi, don't start rumors." Harper paused. "Were you with Sadie this morning?"

"No, this evening, why?" Heidi asked. "We didn't have a dress fitting, did we?"

"No, but Chris seemed to think we did."

Heidi went silent for a beat, then she sighed. "He came over? For crying out loud! He's not supposed to *see* the dress—"

"He didn't come in. He talked to Gabe outside."

"And what did he say?" Heidi pressed.

"I'm more curious about why you're lying to him," Harper retorted.

"I'm not lying—Okay, maybe a tiny bit. But these are my last few months of freedom, Harper. You don't know what it's like to be engaged."

"Oh, the misery," Harper replied with an eye roll. "A handsome, successful guy wants to marry you. My heart bleeds. So where were you?"

"If I tell you, you can't get all mother hennish on me."

"Since when do I get mother hennish?" Harper snapped. "Just tell me."

"I was having a coffee with Trent."

"Your ex," Harper muttered.

"He's perfectly safe," Heidi said, an eye roll evident her tone, too. "Chris is a step up from Trent, and you know it. Besides, Trent's wife is expecting their second any day now. He's a married father of almost two."

"And he's having coffee with you."

"He was congratulating me!" Heidi snapped. "People can have a friendly coffee. Seriously, Harper, I don't need to be babysat."

"And if there was nothing wrong with it, why did you lie to your fiancé?" she shot back.

"Trent needs a new job. He was hoping that the Holmeses might have an opening. So it was innocent. But Chris has been…I don't know. Clingy lately. He wants to do everything together. Ever since I put on this ring, it's like we're joined at the hip."

"Like a married couple would be," Harper said.

"Except we aren't married yet," Heidi replied. "And I just want a little space."

Harper sighed. This was the same old Heidi. Even with the wealthiest bachelor in the county wanting to marry her. "You did the same thing to Trent."

"I did not!"

"You did. You dumped him because he wanted too much from you."

Heidi sighed. "I'm not dumping Chris. I'm just enjoying what freedom I have left. That's it."

Freedom. As if planning a life with the man she loved was some sort of hardship. Granted, the Holmes family was prominent and wealthy, so there would be some new pressures that Heidi wasn't used to…but still!

Harper couldn't lecture, though. She'd done enough of that with Andrea, and she'd learned from it. Life was hard, messy and complicated, and Harper might heartily disagree with someone else's choices, but she had no right to dictate.

"Heidi, Chris knows you lied to him," Harper said quietly. "I just thought you should know that."

"All right. Thanks. I'd better call him."

"Heidi, is the wedding on?" Harper asked seriously. "Because I'm about to cut Grandma's dress here—"

"Yes," Heidi said firmly. "Of course, it's on. I'll work it out with Chris. You know I love him."

"Okay…" And it did make Harper feel a little better. She didn't want her sister to cast aside another good man. She deserved happiness, too. "He's a good guy, Heidi. A really good guy."

"I know. And he puts up with me." Heidi sounded a little bashful. "I shouldn't have lied. I know that. Let me call him."

"Okay. Talk to you later."

After Harper hung up, she rubbed her hands over her face. Chris was in love with Heidi, even with her faults. But this was what a relationship was—forgiving each other, trying to understand each other, and taking the bumps as well as the smooth parts of the road. When Chris had proposed to Heidi, Harper had felt in her core that her sister had a very good man.

And Harper would not allow petty jealousy to put a wedge between her and her sister.

Father, help me to be happy for her. Your blessings aren't limited, and Your plans for me aren't any less because You have plans for other people, too.

What good was a wedding dress to Harper with no groom? Heidi was getting married first, and Harper would have to make her peace with that. But looking back on her sister's wedding ten years from now, or even twenty, she didn't want to be ashamed of herself.

Harper picked up the shears and crossed the kitchen to the hanging dress. She lifted the fabric and held it taut between her fingers.

"Here we go…" she murmured, and sucking in a deep breath, she opened the scissors and made the first, bold cut. The blades sliced through lace, the threads popping apart with the whisper of metal sliding against metal. Now it was begun, and there was no going back.

She might as well hem this dress to her sister's specifications.

This was no longer Grandma's dress, or even Harper's. It was Heidi's.

In the bedroom of the Camdens' bed and breakfast, Gabe tucked some clothing on top of the box into his suitcase, as if layers of clothing could somehow make it disappear from his thoughts, too.

Of all places for the sensitivity training, Comfort Creek was the worst choice possible—at least, for Gabe. For anyone else, it was just a small town. And if he'd been sent to some other little town to think about his behavior, he'd have been able to endure it.

That night, he slept fitfully, dreaming of familiar streets that led nowhere and friends he hadn't seen in years. He woke up tired and irritable. Even Lily's breakfast of pancakes and sausages did little to lift his mood. He'd been avoiding his hometown for this very reason. He wasn't ready to face it all, and yet he didn't have much choice. He was here in Comfort Creek until his training was up, and when he did drive away, he'd be leaving a four-year-old daughter behind.

Driving away from his daughter—that thought had started to ache in a dull, uncomfortable way. Shaking the dust off his shoes wouldn't be quite so simple anymore.

Just as he was leaving the bed and breakfast, Gabe got a call on his cell phone from the chief.

"What can I do for you, sir?" Gabe asked.

"We've got a hit in Fort Collins on some of the articles stolen from Blessings Bridal," Chief Morgan said. "I'll email the forms, but it's a few tiaras, some…let me see…jeweled belts, and a bridal veil."

Gabe's heart sped up in his chest. "A veil, you say? Is it an old one…like an antique kind of thing?"

"There were a few on the list," the chief said, the clack of a keyboard sounding in the background. "I'm not sure. I wanted you to go down to the pawn shop and check it out since you're part of the FCPD. It's just simpler that way."

"Yeah, sure, no problem." Gabe perked up at the chance to head back home, even for a couple hours. Maybe it would help him feel more like himself again.

"Thanks, Gabe. I'll need a full report when you get back."

As Gabe hung up the phone, he felt a smile tickling the corners of his lips. A lead—finally. His time in Comfort Creek could count for more than discipline.

When Gabe drove back into Comfort Creek later that day, he was satisfied. He'd collected several items from the list of stolen property at that pawn shop, pumped as much information from the owner as he could, and left his card for the man to call him if he remembered anything else. Gabe wasn't holding his breath on that one.

And for once, he was actually glad to be heading back to Comfort Creek because he had something that Harper wanted, and he could be the guy who handed it over.

Blessing Bridal was open for business when he parked his squad car out front. He was in uniform this time, and when he hopped out of his car and headed to the front door, a few people did a double take, watching him pull open the front door. It felt good to be in uniform again—the crisp dark blue, the gun at his side, the bulletproof vest. It was like a shield between him and the emotional turmoil he was so tired of dealing with. In this uniform, he was defined—a cop, a protector, a law enforcer. He knew who he was dressed like this. In plainclothes, he wasn't so sure of himself.

The store was empty of customers, and Harper stood behind the counter, looking at a binder, her finger moving down a page. She was dressed in a soft cream-colored sweater. The overhead bell jingled cheerfully, and she looked up. She smiled when she saw him, straightening.

"Where've you been?" Harper asked. "I thought you were supposed to be my personal bodyguard, or something."

"I still am," he said with a short laugh. "The chief asked me to retrieve a few things from a pawn shop in Fort Collins." He lifted a large bag that he carried at his side. "Thought you might be interested in that."

"You found some of my merchandise?" she asked, her expression brightening. "Really?"

Harper came out from behind the counter, and Gabe put down the canvas bag and then pulled it open. He took out several tiaras and the crystal encrusted belts one by one—carefully so as not to ruin them. Harper took each one, running her fingers over the crystals almost reverently.

"This one's damaged," she said with a sigh. "But the others are in good shape."

"And there were a couple of veils, too," Gabe said, pulling the first veil from the bag. It was wrapped in paper to protect it, and he saw Harper's breath catch as she eased the tape back.

"The Irving veil." She smiled and nodded. "This is an expensive piece. I know that insurance can replace most of it, but it will take some time. I'd rather just have the originals."

"One more." This time, he pulled out a pale pink box, and Harper's eyes immediately misted. Her lips trembled as she reached for the box.

"You found it…" she breathed, and she pulled off the lid and lifted out a creamy colored veil, topped with aged pink rosettes. She checked it over from top to bottom, her fingers moving across the delicate fabric. "Oh, Gabe!"

Harper put the veil back into the box and flung her arms around his neck. Gabe had been expecting to please her, but not quite like this—and before he could think better of it, he slid his arms around her waist and pulled her close. She smelled of something soft and floral, and she felt warm and perfect in his arms—so perfect that he wished he could just bury his face in her neck and hold her there, but he wasn't that foolish. He released her after a moment, but instead of stepping back to a safe distance, she looked up into his face, her glittering green eyes searching his.

"How did you find it?" she whispered almost con-spiratorially.

"It was reported by the Fort Collins department," he

said, his voice low in response to her whisper. "And I... uh...went to get it for you."

"I can't believe I have it back..." She wiped an errant tear from her cheek. "Just last night, I was working on my sister's wedding dress and doing some praying, and—let's just say this is a God thing, you know what I mean? I feel like this is confirmation that everything will be okay."

It had been a long time since he'd felt like everything would be okay.

"I envy you that," he said quietly. "But I'm glad you have it back with the family, where it belongs."

There was a spot of color in her pale cheeks. She nudged her glasses up over the freckles on her nose, and she smiled gratefully.

"Thank you, Gabe. I mean, really. Thank you so much. This veil...it was more than just a veil. It represented something more personal to me—my future, I suppose. My own chance at happiness. And I'm sure you don't want to hear about a girl's hopes and dreams, and how they never quite died, but...this means the world..."

And while she prattled on with her thanks, he felt a wave of awkward discomfort. He didn't know how to respond to gratitude—especially hers. He just wanted her to stop talking, and while he looked down at those pink lips, he could think of one way of making that happen.

"Harper." He stepped closer, and instead of retreating, she tipped her chin up, meeting his gaze easily. "I—" He had no words. He was glad to have brought this back to her—to have given her something that mattered. But in the midst of that, he was feeling something much deeper, something almost painful. All he wanted was to kiss her.

"You're a good man, Gabe," Harper said quietly.

But he wasn't. He was a man, certainly, but not a good one. He was a lost man, a frustrated man. He was now a father set up to disappoint his only daughter. He disappointed every woman who got too close, but if he was going to let a woman down, he'd rather it be with emotional honesty than pretending he was something he wasn't.

And those beautiful lips, parted again as she drew in a breath to keep talking, were all he could think about. They were all he'd been able to think about for days now.

"I try real hard," he said gruffly, and he dipped his head down and caught her lips with his—anything else she was about to say evaporating on her tongue. He felt a rush of relief to have finally closed that distance be-tween them. He put a hand up to her face and kissed her gently as her eyes fluttered shut, and for just a mo-ment, she sank against his chest. The store melted away around them as his lips moved over hers, and he felt her soft sigh against his face. Then she stiffened and pulled back.

"Gabe..." Her fingers moved to her lips, touching them as if burned.

"Sorry," he said with a small smile. "I've been want-ing to do that ever since I saw you again."

"But—" She dropped her hand.

And he bent down and kissed her lips again. He was going to regret this—he knew that for a fact—so he might as well kiss her again. It could count as one big mistake. But this time as his lips met hers, she kissed him back, and his heart sped up at the realization. She felt this, too—it wasn't one-sided this time around. And while he knew he had very good reasons to be keeping a distance from this woman, he couldn't quite remember them with her in his arms. She was so warm and soft and fragrant, and every single hope he'd held over the years seemed to tumble back into the room.

The bell above the door jingled and they both startled. Harper leaped from his arms. A blush blazed over her cheeks, and her scandalized gaze swept from Gabe to the newcomer.

"Heidi," Harper squeaked. "Hi…"

"Oh!" Heidi pulled off her sunglasses and ran a hand through her short-cropped, auburn hair. "I didn't mean to disturb…"

"Shut up," Harper said irritably. "You aren't. Gabe was just leaving."

That was a dismissal all right, and he shot Harper a roguish smile. "Fine, I'll go. Have a good afternoon, ladies."

He passed Heidi, who stared at him in unveiled curiosity as she came inside the store, and he pulled open the door, his heart still beating faster than normal. He needed a blast of leaf-scented air to get his brain back on track. Then he could figure out what on earth he'd just done in there…and how bad he'd regret it. Because right now in the moment, he didn't regret a thing. He'd meant that kiss.

"Gabe?" Harper called after him, and he turned back, the outside breeze tugging at him.

Harper's green eyes were fixed on him, and her cheeks still bloomed pink. It took all his self-restraint not to stride back in there and kiss her all over again—

audience or not. But he'd done enough dumb things for one day, and he was pretty sure he'd be kicking himself for this later as it was.

"Yeah?" he said.

"Thanks again—for the veil."

"All part of the job," he said, but he caught her gaze for a millisecond, and he saw so much more swimming beneath the surface—emotions he had no right to decipher.

Gabe turned again, then headed out the door and into the street. He might have been an idiot to have kissed her to begin with, but *she'd kissed him back*!

Chapter Ten

❧

"What was that!" Heidi said as the door shut behind Gabe.

Harper rubbed her hands over her hot cheeks and shut her eyes in a grimace. "I don't know."

"You do know!" Heidi retorted. "Kissing your police protection?"

"He just came to drop off a few things, and—" Harper shrugged helplessly. "He kissed me first for the record."

Heidi grinned. "This is good for you. You're too cautious all the time. Take a risk. Have some fun. My fun days are over, so you'll have to do it for me."

Harper shot her sister a sharp look. "No, this isn't good for me. He's Zoey's father, you'll recall. Zoey needs two functional parents in her life, and the one thing we have going for us is that we aren't exes. Besides, he doesn't want the life I do. I've known that from the start."

"He's Zoey's dad—what could be more perfect?" Heidi countered.

"He's not her father because he *wanted* her," Harper

replied with a shake her head. "He's the same guy he was when he was with Andrea. He even told me that finding out about Zoey wouldn't have sealed the deal for him and Andrea."

"You told him—"

"I did." Harper sighed. "I don't want to argue about that, either. It was the right thing to do."

Heidi put up her hands in silent retreat.

"He doesn't want this, Heidi," Harper went on. "And I do! I want a husband, kids, the white picket fence. Just like you—"

Heidi looked away, chewing the side of her cheek.

"What?" Harper prodded.

"Did he find Grandma's veil?"

"Yes." Harper picked it up from the counter. "Safe and sound. I'm bringing it home tonight so we can keep it somewhere safer than here in the store."

Heidi nodded, then she looked down at the diamond solitaire on her hand. Harper knew that look…she'd seen it so many times with her sister.

"Heidi, what's going on?" Harper asked, softening her tone.

"I think I made a mistake, Harper." Tears misted her sister's eyes. "A big one."

"You mean lying to Chris?" Harper asked uncertainly. Please, let it be something so simple!

"I mean in getting engaged." Heidi heaved a sigh. "I talked to him. I told him I was sorry and that I'd gotten together with Trent, and Chris was just furious."

"Do you really blame him?" Harper asked. "A secret coffee with an ex-boyfriend. What if Chris did the same thing with some girl he used to date?"

Heidi spun the ring around her finger, and then

closed her hand into a fist. "I know. I was wrong. I'm not arguing that. It's just—now it begins. We tell each other everything. Any plans, we ask each other first. Any invitations are going to be assumed to be for both of us…"

"This is what you wanted!" Harper exclaimed.

"I thought so." Heidi shrugged.

"I started the alterations on the dress," Harper said hollowly.

"Maybe you should stop," Heidi whispered.

"I took eight inches off the length!" Harper's heart hammered in her throat. "Heidi, I was supporting you, and you told me the wedding was going forward! *I cut the dress*, Heidi!"

Harper's voice was rising in a panic. She'd already sliced the lace apart, re-hemmed the bottom layers… She paused, forcing herself to calm down. Hollering at her sister wasn't going fix anything.

"You're capable of getting caught up in a moment, too," Heidi retorted.

"Do you mean getting engaged to begin with?" Harper pressed. "Are you *really* rethinking this?"

"I don't know," Heidi confessed. "But I've never kissed Chris like *that*."

"Like what?" Harper felt her cheeks heat again. Couldn't they just focus on Heidi's problems and let Harper's stupid mistake melt into the background for once?

"Like you kissed Gabe Banks."

"I thought we clarified that he kissed me." Harper moaned. "Come on, Heidi. That was a stupid mistake. It's done. I'll never do it again."

"Never again? You sure about that?" Heidi asked.

"Because Chris has never pulled me in like that, and I've never melted in his arms like you just did."

"Gabe is tall!" Harper retorted. "It makes it…different, I guess."

Her waist still felt a little chilled from where his arms had been, and the sensation of being held close in his arms was akin to sweeping across a dance floor. He'd been in full control of the moment, nearly lifting her off her feet as his lips had covered hers. And she'd felt the emotion coursing through him—all of his attention, his pent-up, masculine longing, focused on her. She'd never been kissed like that before, either.

"That's what you're standing by?" Heidi asked incredulously. "He's *tall*?"

"I'm saying that I'm sure Chris kisses you just fine!" Harper snapped.

"It isn't his fault," her sister said with a shake of her head. "It takes two to make a kiss like that, doesn't it? And I don't feel like melting in his arms, because…I never have."

"Chris is a good man, Heidi."

"He is," her sister agreed. "But do I love him enough to vow to be his for the rest of my life?"

"You sure thought so before."

"Fine, then explain to me why you turned to melted wax in Gabe's arms, and why that doesn't matter!"

"I—" Harper searched for the words. "Okay, yes, I'm attracted to him. I'm not blind! He's good-looking, he's charming, and he's got this way of opening up around a woman—"

"Around you," Heidi countered.

"Around *women*," Harper said more firmly. "He always was a flirt. He can make any woman feel like that when he focuses his attention on her."

"Except Gabe hasn't been flirting it up with anyone since he got back into town," Heidi said. "I've been chatting with the girls, and there is general disappointment in that area. He's like a statue. He's very polite, don't get me wrong, but that charm? He's been keeping it to himself."

Harper's breath caught in her throat. Could that be true? Gabe Banks had always been the biggest flirt. He could make a woman twice his age giggle—it was appalling. And look what he'd managed with her just a few minutes ago. Although she couldn't blame him. She'd sensed that she was playing with fire there, and she hadn't stepped back. That had been a choice on her part.

"Fine. Maybe he's less of a flirt now," Harper conceded. "But that was just a…a moment. He brought back Grandma's veil and some of the stolen merchandise. I was so grateful, and lately he's been opening up about some personal stuff that is making him more human. It was combination of a few things, I think, and then I hugged him to say thank you, and…"

Harper turned her back on her sister. This was embarrassing enough without having her red cheeks visible.

"What personal things?" Heidi asked.

"It's not mine to talk about," Harper replied. "He trusted me, and that should matter." Besides, she didn't want to be bandying about his painful past. Gabe might not be for her, but he deserved some privacy, too. And for whatever reason, he'd been entrusting her with some really achingly personal memories lately.

"Fine, fine." Heidi put her hands on her hips. "You

were just telling me why this kiss, sparked by a man bringing back a family heirloom and *his vulnerability* didn't matter."

Her sister was teasing her, and Harper knew it, but she wasn't going to be goaded into believing this kiss was anything more than a mutual mistake.

"Feelings don't make for a future, Heidi," Harper retorted. "We're attracted to each other, yes. And we have a spark, a connection. But that doesn't mean that we have any hope of working out. I don't need a flash in the pan, I need a slow burn that will last!"

"And what I wouldn't do for one flash in the pan!" Heidi replied, but this time her voice had lost the teasing and she just sounded sad. "I saw that kiss, Harper, and I don't want to go through my life never being kissed like that…ever. Once I'm married, that's my last chance! My husband will be my source of all romance. And if I signed off on the slow burn, as you put it—"

"Chris loves you," Harper countered.

"I daresay that Gabe loves you, too," Heidi replied.

Harper reached out and caught her sister's hand. "You're spooked. For crying out loud, even I'm a little spooked! That doesn't mean that Chris isn't the man for you. Don't do anything you're going to regret."

"I shouldn't have quit my job for Chris," Heidi said solemnly. "I was more than happy to do it…but that was stupid of me."

"There are other jobs, Heidi, but good men don't come around all that often."

Heidi squeezed her sister's hand back, and her chin trembled a little. "I have a cake tasting with my future mother-in-law. I can't be late."

As Harper watched her sister leave the store, her

heart filled with regrets of her own. What had she done? And by giving in to whatever chemistry had been brewing between her and Gabe, had she just knocked her sister off balance?

Her sister's words were thrumming through her head. *I daresay Gabe loves you, too...*

Lord, am I leading Gabe on?

That was her worry. She'd kissed him back—and she shouldn't have. She'd put herself into this situation, allowed herself to be swept along with whatever they were feeling in the moment. She'd been the voice of reason for Andrea, and now Harper was making the same mistake! Harper had no right to let him kiss her. They had no future together. She'd been wrong.

Harper picked up her cell phone from the counter and dialed Gabe's number. The phone rang twice, and then his voice mail answered: "Hi, this is Gabe Banks. Leave me a message."

She hung up and heaved a sigh.

Whatever was growing between them needed to be stamped out now, before anyone got hurt. Because while the adults were pussyfooting around each other, Zoey would be the one to suffer. That little girl needed two parents who loved her, and who could be supportive coparents. Mixing up an emotional mess wasn't fair to her!

Harper was a mother now, and her daughter had to take priority. Heidi was wrong—a passionate kiss meant nothing. A ring on her finger and a decent man who loved her—Heidi had it better than she realized.

Heidi needed to recognize that the grass wasn't greener on the other side. Harper was free as a bird, and she'd trade places with her sister in a heartbeat. Greener grass was just a trick of the light.

* * *

Gabe slowed as he passed Blessings Bridal for the umpteenth time the next morning. He was patrolling… and keeping his distance. He'd made a fool of himself the day before, and he was being a coward right now, trying to avoid facing Harper.

The night before, he'd done a whole lot of thinking. He'd sat on the porch of the Camdens' bed and breakfast, a black coffee in one hand and his Bible resting on his knee. And he'd prayed like he'd never prayed before.

Lord, we both know she's not right for me. Take away whatever this is that I'm still feeling for her. Make this easier.

But God wasn't answering that prayer—at least not with a yes. Maybe this was like patience—a virtue only gained through experience. But he'd made this mistake with Andrea, too—let himself get too close to a good woman that he'd never be good enough for. And heartbreak ensued. As always.

Gabe took a left, scanning the cars on the street. He was almost certain that the robbers would be observing the store, and they were likely hiding in plain sight. So patrolling in an unmarked car without his uniform was the best he could do. The clock was ticking on his time here in Comfort Creek, and while he was anxious to get back home again to Fort Collins, he didn't want to leave without closing this case. The Comfort Creek PD was good and all, but Gabe wasn't about to leave Harper and Zoey's safety in the hands of a small-town department whose specialty was *feelings*, of all things.

His goal was to wrap up this robbery case, say his goodbyes, and do what he knew he had to.

The most cutting things his grandmother had ever

said to him were the things he couldn't deny. Like when she told him that he was the kind of kid who, when faced with two choices, would choose the wrong one every time. She'd been right, for the most part. That's why he was here.

He couldn't keep that cycle going. This time around, he needed to make the right choice, even if it went against his first instincts…because his instincts tended to be dead wrong when it came to personal relationships. He needed to keep to his strengths—law enforcement.

Gabe circled back around to Sycamore Drive, and as he drove past Good Eatin', a mom-and-pop-style restaurant, he recognized the blaze of Harper's curls in the window. She was eating a sandwich of some sort, and he signaled, then parallel parked out front.

He'd been avoiding her calls since yesterday, praying for guidance. It was probably time to face her. Besides, he had to grudgingly admit that he missed her, even after this short time. And if he didn't lay things out straight, he'd probably slip up again. He knew himself. He needed to face whatever he was feeling for her head on, or he'd never be free of it.

Gabe got out of the car and headed for the front door of the restaurant. He held the door open for an older couple that was just exiting, then went inside. Harper was still seated by the window, a book open in front of her, and a grilled cheese sandwich held aloft between her fingertips. It didn't make things easier when a greasy sandwich made her even more beautiful.

"Hi," Gabe said, sliding into the bench across from her. Harper looked up in surprise.

"Gabe!" She put down the sandwich on the plate and

licked her fingers. Then her expression clouded. "I've been calling you."

"I know." He winced. "I'm sorry, Harper. I had to think—get my head on straight."

She nodded, but didn't answer.

"Then I saw you in the window, and figured maybe it was a sign."

"A sign about what?" she asked skeptically.

"I don't know…that I needed to just face you." He smiled cajolingly.

Harper nodded, slid a bookmark into place and let her book fall shut. It looked like poetry—a well-worn volume.

"Am I disturbing you?" He was relatively sure he was. What woman liked having her reading time violated?

"It's okay. The store is closed for lunch, and I'm just having a bite before I go to a meeting at the bank."

"The bank, huh?"

"I'm getting a loan for Blessings Maternity."

Harper would get that loan, no doubt, and go on to tell Zoey that the sky was the limit. As he looked at her—those thoughtful green eyes, the tangle of fiery curls, the lips pursed in an expression of caution—he knew that Harper could give his daughter far more than he ever could. She could be an example of life lived well, the "mama" in her little life that Gabe had never had.

"About before—" Harper licked her lips. "The kiss, I mean. That can't happen anymore, Gabe."

"Yeah, for sure. Look, that was on me. I—" How could he explain what it felt like to look down into those green eyes, to have her lips close enough to catch with his own… "I guess I was just caught up in the moment."

"Me, too." She sighed. "But we aren't teenagers any-more, and there's a lot more to lose now."

"You think this is about what I felt for you back then?" He squinted, then shook his head. "Harper, I definitely had a thing for you, but come on… It's been over ten years."

Color tinged her cheeks. "So what was it, then?"

He met her gaze, and his heart clenched in his chest. "That's how I feel about you now."

Harper blinked, then dropped her gaze. She picked up a napkin and began to carefully wipe her fingers. Great. He'd just made her uncomfortable. But it was true. He wasn't some creep nursing a crush from when he was a kid. She was fully able to pull him in right now, with both of them being adults and knowing ex-actly why it wouldn't work. And that was the problem.

"Harper…" He lowered his voice. "I know I over-stepped, okay?"

"You did," she confirmed.

"But you also kissed me back." He quirked up one side of his mouth. "Just to be fair."

The pink in her cheeks deepened and she shot him an annoyed look. "Maybe I did. But I shouldn't have."

"Granted." He nodded. "You should have slapped me across the face and thrown me out. Although, I have to say, it was a little bit gratifying to know it wasn't one-sided this time around. A guy's ego can only take so much." She smiled, and he felt a surge of relief. He needed to patch this up. "I've been really struggling, trying to come to terms with Zoey being mine and all that, and I've come to a realization."

Harper met his gaze, pressing her lips together as she waited for him to continue.

"I always knew I wouldn't make much of a family man. I've got my own issues to sort out, and Andrea wasn't the only woman to be disappointed in what I had to offer." Gabe shook his head. "They say when you become a parent, the child has to come first, and I'm going to do that. I'm Zoey's dad."

"You aren't going to—" the color drained from Harper's face "—take her back to the city with you…"

"No, no!" He reached out and put a hand over hers without thinking. "Harper, she's better off with you. I can see that. What could I offer her in the city? Daycare, babysitters and a father who has no idea what he's doing? While I might have a few grudges against this town, I can see that she's happy here with you, and that you'd do anything to keep her safe. What more could a kid want?"

"Her father." Harper's eyes misted. "She's going to need you in her life, you know."

"I know," he agreed. "And I'll be around—just in the distance. I'll send presents at the appropriate times, come visit once in a while. Maybe you could bring her out to the city and we could spend some time together when it's convenient for you. I never planned to be a father, and having found out about Zoey doesn't change the reasons."

Harper was silent for a moment. "What if she wants to talk to you?"

"You'll have my number. I'll be there."

"And when she starts dating?" Harper smiled sadly.

"I'll make a special trip out here to meet the young man and put some healthy fear in him."

"Have I chased you off, then?"

"No." Gabe leaned back in the seat. "I just see myself making the same mistakes I always did, and it's time to put a stop to it."

"Me. I'm the mistake."

"Look, I'm the idiot who keeps convincing myself that something can work when it obviously can't. I'm not a family man, and you want a family. You *have* a family. You were right that Zoey has to come first, and I can't go messing up my friendship with you."

"Zoey's grandparents aren't thrilled with me for telling you about her," Harper said. "But I want you to know that I will never block you from your daughter's life. In fact, I might hound you a little when she needs her dad."

"You're a good person, Harper," he said quietly.

"So are you, Gabe."

Not as good as he wished he could be. He knew he was letting Harper down right now, but it was better to do it earlier, before emotions were invested.

"So we're okay?" he asked cautiously.

"Yes." Harper nodded. "We'll make sure that Zoey grows up to be secure, happy and confident. And when she graduates from high school, I want you at my side so we can celebrate that milestone together. Is it a deal?"

"Deal." Gabe reached across the table and took her hand, intending to shake on it, but her soft skin slowed him down, and he held her fingers in his. He swallowed, then released her. "In the meantime, I'm going to do my best to catch those morons who broke into your store so you won't have to worry about them anymore. I have a few more days."

"Thank you. I appreciate that." She smiled. "I'll sleep better when I'm not worried about another break-in."

"You and me, both," he muttered, then he rose from his seat. "I'll let you finish your lunch. I'm on patrol."

Harper nodded, and he turned for the door. When he got there, he glanced back and found her still staring at him with a perplexed look on her face. One creamy hand lay on top of the book, and her lips were pursed as if she was deep in thought.

Why couldn't this be easier? Why couldn't seeing her again have put it all into perspective for him so that he didn't feel like he was getting torn in two every time he tried to make the right choice?

But this time, he *would* make the right choice. His heart had to be overruled in this situation—his daughter was too important to take any risks with. Harper was everything in a mother that he'd ever wanted for himself. Zoey would be loved, cherished, guided and nurtured. She'd be *fine*, and definitely better off without him too close to mess her up.

Gabe would keep this county safe for Zoey. It might not be much, and his daughter would eventually judge him for all he *didn't* do, but it was the best he could offer.

Chapter Eleven

Harper sat in front of her half-finished sandwich, her mind spinning. Her appetite was gone, and while she'd managed to pull off a self-assured and competent air, she didn't feel quite so confident now that Gabe was gone.

What had she expected when she sprung paternity on this man? She'd been the one to repeatedly warn her friend that Gabe wasn't going to give her what she wanted…so why was Harper feeling this overflow of disappointment that he wasn't stepping up now?

He wasn't the husband and father sort of guy—and it wasn't Zoey's responsibility to change her father. But Harper realized that against all logic, she'd started to hope for more from Gabe.

"It's my own fault," she muttered to herself. Well, maybe she could judge Andrea a little less harshly now that she could see how easy it was to make this particular mistake.

Besides, wasn't this the outcome she'd been expecting from the beginning—that he'd walk away and she could go back to raising Zoey with a clear conscience?

Yet somewhere along the way, she'd started to see Gabe in a new light. He wasn't just a womanizer, he was a wounded man who'd never been properly loved by his grandmother. He wasn't selfish as much as scarred. It wasn't that he didn't feel anything; if anything, Gabe felt things too deeply and didn't think he had enough to give back. She was sympathizing with him, when right now she should be straightening her shoulders and getting ready to face the challenges that were bound to come up.

Judging Gabe was easier when he was nothing more than a caricature, the type of man to avoid. But over the last week, he'd become so much more. He was…a friend. And she realized that she respected him now, where she never had in the past. He was a Christian, and that showed. He wasn't playing the field anymore, and he wasn't misrepresenting himself, either. Her hopes weren't his fault.

"Anything else today?" the waitress asked, pulling Harper out of her thoughts. Harper looked down at her watch.

"No, thanks. I have an appointment. I'll just pay at the counter, if that's okay with you."

"Sure thing. Have a good day!"

Harper pulled out her credit card to pay. She needed to get herself re-centered before her meeting at the bank. Not everything was about Gabe, and that included Blessings Maternity. Maybe even *especially* Blessings Maternity. This new store was about the future she was working toward, not some misplaced emotions that she was bound to regret later. Her head had to lead with this goal.

Lord, please help me to get this loan, she prayed in her heart. She didn't need a man to complicate her life.

She didn't need Gabe hanging in too close to distract her from what really mattered, either. So Gabe going back to his life in the city was for the best, even if it stung in a strangely deep part of her heart. What she needed right now was financing for her newest business venture—a step toward a comfortable future with her little girl.

Forty-five minutes later, Harper came out of the bank and onto the leaf-strewn sidewalk, her heart pounding with excitement. She'd just secured a nice healthy loan for Blessings Maternity! She wanted to jump and squeal, but that wouldn't be dignified. So she grinned to herself and clutched her folder closer to her chest, allowing herself one little skip as her shoes crunched over the dry leaves that fluttered down from the trees. *Thank You, Lord!* she prayed. Blessings Maternity would be a reality. She'd been planning the details for her store for a long time now, and she knew the suppliers she wanted to use, the way the store would look, even the sign—subtly linked to the Blessings Bridal logo. She could see it all in her mind's eye, and with the funding arranged, it felt so much more concrete. This was actually happening!

Harper pulled her phone out of her pocket, eager to call someone to share the joy of the moment. The first person to pop into her head was Gabe, and she sighed. What was wrong with her? But the image of Gabe tugged at her heart, all the same. He reminded her of what she was missing in her life—the thrill of new feelings, of romance, of kisses that should never have happened… She was missing out on that wedding of her own—the one she'd been mentally planning since she was ten.

But so far, God hadn't brought along the right guy, and Harper would rather count the blessings she did have than regret the blessings that weren't hers yet. While Harper didn't have a husband of her own, she did have a family. And not every family looked the same. That was just life! She was a mom now, and she had her dad, her sister, and soon Chris would be part of the mix.

And she knew exactly who would celebrate this moment with her. Harper dialed her dad's number and angled her steps across the street while it rang. Her dad was the one man who would fully understand what this meant to her.

"Hi, Harper," her father said as he picked up. "So how did it go?"

"I got the loan!" She waved at a truck that slowed to let her cross, then hopped up on the opposite curb, tugging her wrap a little closer against the chilly breeze.

"That's my girl!" her father thrilled. "Good for you! I knew it would work out—I could feel it in my bones. But I'm still glad to hear it! So how much will they lend you? And what's the interest rate?"

Harper went through the details with her father—the only one who could truly appreciate those finer points of the loan. Her heels tapped a cheerful rhythm against the sidewalk, and she nodded at an older woman she knew from church on her way past. This was still private news, but she couldn't help the smile on her face.

"It sounds really good. That's a competitive rate," her father said, and she could almost feel him nodding through the phone. "What are you going to do to celebrate?"

"I don't know," she admitted. "I was just going to start looking for commercial spaces for lease—"

"Harper, come on," her father chuckled. "You can't work every spare minute. You've got to do something to celebrate. You've put a lot of work into this business plan, and the bank believes in you, too. You need to cut loose a bit."

"I will," she promised with a low laugh.

"So where are you headed now?"

"Back to the store, of course," Harper said. "I need to find another employee. We need a full-timer, Dad. I know it's more expensive with benefits and all that, but with the new store, I'm going to need a full staff in both places, and part-timers just aren't as reliable."

"That's fair enough," her father agreed. "But more immediately, have the police seen any suspicious activity around the store?"

"Gabe has been patrolling, as well as the rest of the police department, and so far nothing," Harper said. "Maybe whoever hit the store won't come back."

"Maybe." Her father's voice deepened.

"You don't sound convinced."

"I'm worried about you, Harper. You're working so hard, raising Zoey, and now our store is targeted by thieves. I just want you to stay safe. Merchandise can be replaced. Daughters, not so much."

"You don't need to worry about me, Dad," she said, softening. "I'm fine. Besides, Gabe seems to be taking this one seriously. I told you that they found some of the merchandise, including Grandma's veil, right?"

"Yes, you did." Her father sighed. "You're in good hands. I know that, Harper. But I don't want anything happening to you, so keep your eyes open, okay? If something seems off, or weird, listen to your gut."

"Always, Dad. I'd better get going. I'm almost at the store."

"All right. Talk to you later."

Harper hung up her phone and dropped it into her bag as she approached her shop. Fluffy clouds sailed overhead and a golden sunlight splashed down onto the street, warming Harper against the brisk wind.

She rummaged in the bottom of her bag for her keys and pulled them out. The first thing she did was snatch down the Back in One Hour sign she'd posted when she'd left the store, but as she slid the key into the lock, she noticed something that stopped her heart in her chest.

There were scrapes on the doorjamb and a gouge in the wood of the door as if someone had tried to pry it open with a crowbar. She stepped back and looked around. A young mother pushed a stroller along the sidewalk on the opposite side of the street, but other than that, there was no one. A pickup truck rumbled to a stop at the four-way stop sign, and she vaguely recognized the old cowboy in the driver's seat. This was Comfort Creek, and she was looking for someone suspicious—it was crazy!

Harper turned the key in the lock and pushed open the door. Everything was in order, and it seemed obvious that whoever had tried to get in had failed.

But they'd *tried*. She shivered and the hair on the back of her neck went up. She suddenly felt very alone standing in this shop, and she knew exactly who she had to call this time. Harper pulled out her phone once more and dialed Gabe's number with a trembling hand. It rang once, then he picked up.

"Hi, Harper. What's up?" He sounded casual enough.

"Gabe, I think they came back." Her voice sounded raspy to her own ears, and she swallowed hard.

"What? What happened?" The casual note to his tone was gone, replaced by professional steel. "Where are you?"

"I'm at the store. There are fresh scrapes on the door. Someone tried to get in while I was away. I was gone for an hour and a half. Maybe an hour and forty-five minutes. But someone was here!"

"I'm two minutes away. Sit tight," he growled. "Is anyone around?"

"I looked. Not really."

"Are you inside the store, or outside?"

"Inside. The door was still locked and there are no broken windows. Everything looks in order, Gabe. I'm probably freaking out for nothing."

She was still rather traumatized from the sight of her trashed store the first time she'd seen it. But looking around at the line of bagged dresses on the racks, the mannequins arrayed in puffy ball gowns, the hardwood floor gleaming in afternoon light—it was reassuringly neat and tidy.

"Step outside the store, lock the door, and wait for me," he ordered.

"I think it's okay," she started. "I'm probably overreacting—"

"Can you just *once* do as I tell you?" he barked.

Harper's nerves tensed at the ice in his voice. Gabe hadn't raised his voice before this. If she wasn't mistaken, he was scared. And if Gabe was scared, she should be, too.

Harper turned on her heel and stepped outside, pulling the door shut behind her.

"Okay. Done. I'm outside," she said, turning the key in the lock again.

"Thank you." His tone was moderated once more. "I'm almost there."

Gabe turned onto Sycamore Drive and picked up the radio.

"This is Officer Banks at Blessings Bridal. I'm going to need backup. Suspected 10-62. Over."

His training was taking over, but underneath that veneer of professional calm, his heart was pounding. This wasn't just any suspected breaking and entering—this was Harper! He'd been waiting for this, and at the same time, he'd been hoping to be by her side when it happened. He wanted to be the barrier between her and any danger that might come. Whoever this was, they were willing to kill to get their way. They had already in Fort Collins.

His siren wailed as he whipped up to the store, and he was relieved to see Harper on the sidewalk with a woolen wrap around her shoulders, fluttering in a rising breeze. She held a folder clutched in front of her chest. Her curls blew around her face and she hitched her shoulders up against the chill. Gabe could hear the incoming sirens already, and he pulled out his gun, keeping it pointed at the ground and clicking off the safety as he approached the front door.

"Gabe," she breathed, and the relief in her voice tugged at him. But he couldn't take the time to reassure her right now. Not until he was certain it wasn't just words.

"Stay outside." He held his other hand out. "Give me the key."

Harper handed it over, her soft fingertips brushing his palm as she did. His nerves were at attention, his skin tingling from her touch as he approached the front door. She was right—someone had definitely tried to get into the store. He unlocked the door, pocketed the key, and silently eased the door open. As he crept inside, the bell overhead jingled, and he inwardly grimaced. He'd forgotten about that.

He was aware that the door hadn't swung shut behind him, and when he turned to see what had blocked it, he came face-to-face with Harper, on his heels. Her eyes were wide and her lips were pale as her gaze whipped around the store.

A wave of anger swept through him. This was no joke, and his first priority was *her* safety. He pointed at her and back to the door, but she just looked at him.

"They could be in here," he whispered. It was a possibility. They were obviously getting brave to come to a town known for its county police presence. He just might have a gun trained on him this very moment, too, so he turned his attention to the sales floor, scanning the racks, the floor, the walls, for any sign of movement or shadow.

"This is the police!" he barked. "Come out with your hands up!"

Silence. He slowed his own breathing, listening for even the smallest sound that might betray someone's presence. He could hear the soft thud of his own heartbeat and Harper's shallow breathing behind him. Satisfied that he could hear nothing else, he made a quick tour of the sales floor, kicking skirts aside as he searched the place, and it was clear. Harper stood at the door where he'd left her, and as he came back toward her, he hissed.

"Outside! Now!"

"There are dresses for two different brides in the back of the store," Harper whispered. "They can't be damaged!"

That was her focus right now? Dresses? Those brides could get married in burlap for all he cared. He shot her a fiery glare and pointed at the outside door once more. At that moment, the door opened again and Bryce Camden appeared, his gun drawn. Good—backup was here.

"Get her out of here," Gabe snapped, and turned toward the back room of the store. He eased his weight onto the balls of his feet, and keeping his gun eye level, crept toward the back room. Behind him, he could hear the whispered conversation as Bryce encouraged Harper to get back outside and let the professionals do their work. It bugged him, because he couldn't focus the way he should with her in the store. It was like part of his mind kept slipping back to where she stood by the door.

If anyone's body armor should be standing between her and danger, it should be his. But he couldn't do everything at once.

The back room was neatly arranged—shelves lined with boxes, rolls of ribbon and various sewing accoutrements. There was nowhere to hide back here, and the rear door was solidly shut—locked with a sliding bolt from the inside. No one had exited the store. He let out a breath of relief, slid the safety lock on his gun and holstered it.

"Clear back here!" Gabe called and returned to the sales floor. Bryce holstered his weapon, too, and they eyed each other for a moment.

"What was that?" Bryce said. "A message? Just toying with us? Testing our response time?"

"Or an actual attempt to get inside?" Gabe wondered aloud. "Maybe whoever it was got interrupted."

Bryce shook his head. "They're around—we know that much."

"And they're watching," Gabe added. "Harper had left for lunch and an appointment. She had a sign up saying how long she'd be gone. And they managed to do that damage on the door outside without anybody noticing—at least no one that called it in."

"We'll do a canvass of the area and see if anyone remembers anything," Bryce said.

Gabe headed for the front door just as four more officers arrived on the scene. Harper stood outside, her wrap pulled close around her shoulders and her glittering green gaze pinned to him.

"Nothing," he confirmed. "The store is empty. The back door is secured. No one got inside."

Harper exhaled a sigh. "I thought so."

"Better safe than sorry," he said. He hadn't meant to scare her, but they weren't playing games with this one…and neither were the crooks.

Gabe looked back at the gouges on the door frame. Someone had put some muscle into that, and the thought made the hair on the back of his neck bristle. There was no mistake—whoever had broken in earlier was definitely back…or had never left. Harper—or at the very least her store—was being watched.

"You should close the store for a few days," Gabe said. "Just take a step back. I'll keep an eye on you, but the store is obviously under surveillance."

"When the store is closed, I lose money."

"I know." He could sympathize with that. "But these are extenuating circumstances. I think you can agree to that."

Harper nodded slowly. "I hate this, Gabe…being run out of my own store. We have a living to make, too, and this isn't just about stealing our merchandise anymore. This is about stealing my sense of security!"

"As long as I'm with you, you're secure enough," he said, then glanced around at the arriving officers. "Let's let the officers here do a sweep of the neighborhood. You'll want to pick up Zoey anyway, won't you?"

Harper gave him a peculiar look, and he could only guess at what she was thinking. But yes, he was worried about his daughter, too. He wanted both of them under his watch tonight, if only to make himself feel better.

"Okay," Harper agreed. "That's a good idea. She's at the daycare on Elm Street. The one with the puzzle piece sign."

"Good."

"Ms. Kemp," one of the officers said, coming up. "We'll need a statement—"

"She's with me," Gabe interrupted. "Give me the form. I'll walk her through it and hand it in myself."

"Sure thing."

The officer retreated, and Gabe slipped a hand over her slim elbow, tugging her in closer to his body. He felt better when she was beside him, because he could protect her more easily this way. And if any of those criminals were watching right now, he wanted them to know that she wasn't alone. He might be undercover, but he was still a very large man. If they crossed her, they crossed *him*.

"We need Zoey's booster seat," Harper said.

Of course—he hadn't even thought of it. They'd get the booster seat, pick up their daughter, and then get them both home to where they were safe. His time here in Comfort Creek was limited, and there was no way he could walk away from this frustrating town without having arrested whoever was responsible for the break-in.

Then he could wash his hands of this place and go deal with his emotions in Fort Collins, where he belonged.

Chapter Twelve

Gabe glanced over at Harper as she put on her seat belt. She still looked pale, and her hands trembled just a little as the buckle found its home.

"You okay?" he asked, starting the car. He just wanted to get her away from here—let the other officers do their jobs.

"Hmm."

It wasn't actually an answer, and he reached over and took one of her chilled hands in his. He gave her fingers a squeeze.

"It's natural to be a little shaken," he said.

"But why are they targeting me?" she asked, turning toward him, and her fingers twined through his. She didn't seem to have noticed what she'd done, and he didn't have the heart to pull his hand back. Her eyes brimmed with unshed tears.

"It's not personal," he said with a shake of his head. "If this is the same gang we think it is, the choice of business to target is pretty random. They're looking for fencible merchandise. That's it! This isn't about you doing anything right or wrong. That's why they belong in prison."

"Gabe, they must have been watching me—"

"Did you see anyone?" He pressed. "Anyone at all?"

"A woman with a stroller?" She shrugged feebly. "And no, I didn't know her personally, but she didn't stand out at all."

"It might be an important detail. I'm not sure," he confessed. "But if they want to get to you, they'll have to get through me first. And I have to tell you—I might not be great with authority figures, but I'm real good at hand-to-hand combat."

She smiled wanly, and when she moved to wipe her eyes, she seemed to notice that she'd been holding Gabe's hand.

"Sorry…" she murmured. "I didn't mean to do that…"

"It's okay," he said. It was more than okay. If he could make her feel safe by holding her hand, he'd do it. He'd hold her hand for a whole lot less, truth be told.

Harper wiped her eyes. "I wasn't too scared until you pulled out the gun. I guess it all felt…extra real."

Real. Yeah, it was that. He shot her an apologetic smile. He forgot that most people weren't used to drawn weapons like a trained officer was.

"You—changed," she added. "You're different with a gun."

He chuckled softly. "I tend to give that impression to a lot of people. Even without the gun. But I shouldn't intimidate *you*. You of all people know me. But I hope I scared the pants off of anyone watching you."

She smiled again, then shook her head.

"Thing is, I get that response a lot," he went on as

he started the vehicle. "It's part of what gets me into trouble. I speak my mind, and because I'm a big guy with a deep voice, it comes across as more threatening than I might intend."

She didn't say anything, and Gabe sighed. Confirmation? Some people he didn't mind intimidating. Harper wasn't one of those people. He needed her to see past that defense mechanism—because that's all it was. He pulled away from the curb and eased down Sycamore Street toward Main.

"You're safe with me, you know," he said, softening his voice. "I might be a big lug, but I'll never hurt you, or bully you…or…or… I don't know. I'll never use my size to get my way when it comes to you and Zoey. But I will use it to stand up for the two of you. You can be warned about that in advance."

"I don't need a bodyguard," she said, but he could hear the warmth in her voice.

"Right now you do, actually," he replied. "Look, I know that you'll end up marrying some guy, and I'll slide into the background, but until you have some other guy to throw his weight around for you, if you ever need help—ever—you know that I'm here. Okay?"

He signaled a turn, glancing toward Harper as he eased onto the next street. Her curls hung in ringlets around her face—a few of them wisping away from her head—loosened from the wind outside.

"I'm not so close to getting married as you think," she replied.

"You haven't settled for less than you deserve, and I'm glad. If you turned me down for some guy unworthy of you, I'd take it personally."

She rolled her eyes—at least she was relaxing a bit.

That's what it took—a bit of flirtation? He wished it was as innocent as all that, because when it came to Harper his feelings would always be more complicated.

"Don't tell me you're still smarting from high school," she said.

"Nah." He signaled a turn onto Elm Street. "Not very much, at least."

And he wasn't. This wasn't about high school anymore. He was doing his best to keep his emotions in the clear right now. She was still so very easy to fall for...

The daycare was ahead on the right with a big purple puzzle piece standing out front. He pulled to a stop and turned toward Harper.

"Are you okay, Harper?"

She nodded, then sucked in a deep breath.

"No, I'm serious," he said, reaching out to catch her hand again. "I'm used to that stuff. You aren't."

"Well, I've got you to fend them off, don't I?" she asked with a wan smile. "I'll be fine. But I expect you to fling yourself bodily between me and bad guys."

"Deal." He grinned. "That's the fun part."

Harper's cheeks pinked, and she reached for the door handle. "And maybe you'd stick around for a bit when you drop us off at my place? I'd feel better."

"Also a deal. Let's go get Zoey."

Harper got out of the car first, and Gabe followed her. He met her on the other side and she walked a half step ahead of him as she approached the glass-plated front door. Gabe could see the kids sitting in a circle on a carpet, their hands waving in the air, imitating a middle-aged woman. When they stepped inside, another worker smiled and came over.

"And R is for rumble..." the woman was saying to

the circle of children. "Rumble like the thunder. Can we all rumble?"

Gabe raised his eyebrows, watching the kids do their best to rumble. They were cute, he had to admit, but this was a world that he wasn't used to. Kids were complicated. They needed stuff that he didn't know how to provide. Zoey looked over at them, big gray eyes moving from Harper to Gabe and back again. She waved shyly at him, and he gave her a curt nod in return.

"Hi, Harper," the worker said. "Are you picking up Zoey now?"

"I am." Harper waved at Zoey, and as if that was the signal she was waiting for, she scrambled to her feet and skipped over to them.

"Hi, sweetie," Harper said, running a hand over Zoey's shiny hair. "How was your day?"

"It's good," Zoey replied. "We're doing the letter R today. It's R for rain." She waved her arms in the air in the motion Gabe had seen before. Ah. So that's what it was.

From the circle of children, it seemed that R had moved on to the roar of a bear, and the kids were bellowing into each other's faces in terrorizing delight.

"I like that one…" Zoey said quietly. "I do a good raaaar."

Gabe felt a little self-conscious in this daycare, and he didn't feel comfortable carrying on a conversation with Zoey here. This was Harper's domain—the official space of a mother and her child. He was just some biological interloper. But when he looked down at Zoey, she looked up at him, and just for a moment there was a spark of connection. He understood her desire to roar. A smile curved his daughter's small lips.

"Let's get your coat," Harper said.

"Monday there will be a nature walk," the worker told Harper. "So Zoey will need mittens and a scarf, just in case the temperature drops. Also rubber boots are a plus."

"Will do," Harper agreed. "We'll have to remember that Zoey, okay?"

"Miss Prim? Miss Prim?" Zoey tugged at the young woman's hand.

"Yes, Zoey?" Miss Prim replied, looking down at her.

"That's my daddy."

Gabe's heart seemed to skip a beat, and then hammered hard to catch up. *Daddy.* Had he heard that right? He looked down at Zoey, who was eyeing him shyly, then to the worker whose jaw had literally dropped.

"It's true," Gabe said, clearing his throat. "I'm… uh…her father."

This was only the second person he'd told—the first being Bryce, and that had seemed more like a guilty confession. This—this had been a proud declaration by his daughter.

"Oh…" Miss Prim looked over at Harper, obviously trying to cover up her shock.

"This is Gabe Banks," Harper said with an easy smile. "He's Zoey's biological dad, and she's just met him."

"So a big time for a little girl." The worker was quickly catching up. There was a lot going on between the lines that Zoey didn't need to hear.

"Definitely." Harper smiled over at Gabe, and he cleared his throat. What was the appropriate way to react to all of this? There were expectations, but he had no idea how to fulfill them. Could this end already? Couldn't he just take them home and make sure they were locked in good and tight for the night?

"Does this…change anything for pickups or drop-offs?" Miss Prim asked, lowering her voice. "Because if so, there are forms to be filled out—"

"No, no," Harper said quickly. "Nothing changes."

Nothing changes. Those words stung. He knew she was only referring to their daycare details, but the words struck a little too close to his heart. Wasn't that the plan here—that he'd dash back out again and Zoey would return to her regular routine without him? Not much was *supposed* to change—not with his current plans, at least. And he felt a tug of guilt.

"My daddy's a policeman," Zoey said, digging her toe into the linoleum floor. "And now I got a daddy like Robby's got."

Who was Robby? One of the kids? Likely most of the children had fathers in the picture, and he wondered exactly how much damage he'd already done, simply not knowing about her existence.

He wasn't a daddy. Bryce Camden was a daddy, with his toddler daughter who lit up at the sight of him. So far, Gabe had seen Bryce put his daughter to sleep, feed her breakfast, and he'd heard Bryce cheer through the walls when Emily peed in a potty. That was a dad. Gabe was…an awkward visitor.

"Okay, well, let's go," Harper said with a too bright smile. "Thanks, Miss Prim. We'll see you Monday."

"With mittens and a scarf!" Miss Prim sang back.

Gabe forced a smile and followed Harper and Zoey out the door, holding it open for them from behind until he could get outside to freedom. The daycare suddenly felt stiflingly hot, and he could feel too many eyes on him.

He was a grown man and a cop. He was part of the force that protected all these people, and yet he felt judged. More realistically, he was judging himself.

This is my daddy.

He didn't deserve to be called "daddy." That was a title that was earned.

Harper took off her seat belt after Gabe pulled up to the curb in front of her house. In the back seat Zoey chattered away to herself. She had no idea how much danger her mother was in, and Harper wanted to keep it that way.

"So—" Harper turned to Gabe. "Are you staying for a bit?"

"Sure." His expression softened. "It would make me feel better, too."

"Gabe will stay?" Zoey chimed in from the back seat.

"Yeah, I'll stay for a bit," Gabe replied. "Let's get inside."

"I want to play outside," Zoey countered. "There's new leaves! See, Mommy? There's new ones!"

Harper looked out the window. She'd recently raked up several big bags of leaves, and there was already a new covering of brightly colored leaves across the lawn.

"Yes, I see," she chuckled. "What do you say, Gabe? Are you up to raking leaves into a pile for her to jump in?"

"Uh—" He met her gaze with an uncertain smile. "Sure. That sounds doable."

They got out of the car, and after Zoey's bag was deposited inside the house, Harper headed to the garage to get the rake. Gabe waited outside, his arms crossed over his chest as he surveyed the street.

"What's he doing?" Zoey asked, following her mother through the garage.

"He's—" Harper looked out the garage window to where she could see a sliver of Gabe's muscular arm. "He's waiting for you."

"Is he any good at raking?" Zoey asked.

"Better than me, I'll guess," she replied. "He's got bigger muscles." Harper grabbed the rake from the corner, and shot her daughter a smile. "Go easy on him, would you?"

"What do you mean?" Zoey asked.

"I mean—" How to explain this to a four-year-old? "Maybe be extra nice to him. He didn't know he was a dad before, so he's still learning how this works."

"Oh." Zoey shrugged. "Okay."

For what that was worth! Zoey probably had no idea what Harper even wanted, and frankly, Gabe would just have to learn as he went along, just like every other parent. Sure, he was late to the party, but he'd figure it out.

Harper and Zoey came back outside with the rake, and Harper passed it to Gabe. He accepted it with a rueful grin.

"Everything okay out here?" Harper asked, keeping her voice low.

"As quiet as you'd expect Comfort Creek to be," he replied with a shrug. "Come on, Zoey. Let's start the pile."

The afternoon sun shone down on the yard, warming the day just a little bit. Harper stood back and watched as Gabe raked big swaths of leaves together into a pile and Zoey launched herself into them before they were even worthy of the jump.

"No, no," Gabe laughed. "You've got to wait! Stand there—don't move."

And he raked up another four lines of leaves before Zoey couldn't hold herself back anymore and came careening toward them. Gabe caught her with one arm about six inches above the pile and hauled her back.

"I said wait." He laughed. "You'll see. When the pile is good and big, it'll be way more fun."

Gabe carried Zoey over to Harper and deposited her into Harper's arms. Zoey squealed and laughed, wriggling to be put down.

"Wait!" Harper laughed, and she put Zoey down, but caught her by the coat.

Gabe raked for a couple of minutes—those strong shoulders going to work as he pulled together a pile of crunchy leaves. He raked with a rare enthusiasm she hadn't seen in this man until now. And when he'd gotten most of the leaves into a nice, tall pile, he shot Harper a grin.

"Okay, let her go," he said, and Zoey took off toward the pile with a shriek of delight. She did a belly flop into the center, then flipped over and flailed.

"See?" Gabe said, grinning down at her. "Better, right?"

"Yup!" Zoey agreed. "Do it again!"

Gabe laughed and shook his head. "You're a lot of work, you know."

"I'm worth it!" Zoey shot back, and Harper felt tears mist her eyes. Yes, Zoey was absolutely worth it, and she'd done something right if the girl knew it, too.

"How about you do some raking," Gabe said, handing her the rake.

"No way!" Zoey shook her head. "That's not my job. My job is the jumping. You do the raking."

"What if I want to jump?" Gabe asked with a mock seriousness.

"Tough!" Zoey retorted. "Come on, Gabe! You gotta rake!"

Gabe chuckled and started raking again, this time piling the leaves on top of Zoey, who still lay in the flattened pile.

The next hour went on like that, and Harper took her turn raking, too. When they were done, the yard was no neater than it had been before, but Zoey's cheeks were red with cold and exercise, and Gabe looked a whole lot more relaxed, too. They were getting somewhere, and for a few minutes in the front yard, they'd felt like a family.

Who said they had to be like everyone else? When a mom and a dad loved a little girl—that was a family. And they were getting a start at it.

"I'm cold," Zoey said at last. "Can we have a snack?"

"Sure." Harper turned to Gabe. "Are you coming in?"

Gabe shook his head. "No, I've got more to investigate. I'd better get back to it."

She nodded, a feeling of disappointment washing over her. She liked having Gabe around—but it went deeper than that. It soothed a part of her heart that she hadn't known existed until now. It was the part of her that swelled with warmth when she watched Gabe playing with his little girl in the leaves.

Harper opened the front door for Zoey, and the girl

clattered inside to take off her shoes and coat. Gabe stayed outside.

"Are you staying in tonight?" Gabe asked.

"Why?" Harper asked with a small smile. "Do I have to report that, or something?"

Gabe smiled, but it didn't reach those steely eyes. "I'll put it this way. If you promise to stay in, I'll get more sleep tonight."

Harper swallowed. This was serious, and she shouldn't be joking.

"Yes, we're staying in. We have big plans to bake cookies. My parents are coming by tonight, so..."

Gabe nodded. "Good. That makes me feel better."

"We're making cookies?" Zoey demanded, her little face appearing in the open door behind them.

"Yes, we're making cookies!" Harper chuckled.

"Gabe, are *you* okay?" she asked. He'd relaxed with Zoey in the leaves, but he was looking stony and reserved again.

"Yeah. I'm good." But it wasn't convincing. "I'll patrol your street today, and around your store. You stay home tonight, and hopefully the thieves will try the store again and we'll catch them."

He made it sound so simple. Like picking up pizza. She forced a smile.

"Okay. We'll stay in."

Gabe stepped back onto the grass. "Inside. Locked door. Then I leave."

He had a way of making her feel both safe and uncertain at the same time. She knew that Gabe was going to do whatever it took to keep them out of harm, but something was wrong, and he wasn't opening up.

She didn't have much choice, though, so she stepped

inside and scooped up Zoey's coat from the floor where she'd left it. When Harper looked back, Gabe hadn't moved a muscle—arms crossed over that broad chest. He looked...sad.

She raised a hand in a wave. "Thank you, Gabe."

"Yeah. No problem."

Harper closed the door and slid the deadbolt into place, then looked out the window to see Gabe headed back toward his car. Gabe wasn't okay, but he was putting it aside to take care of them.

"Mommy?" Zoey's voice pulled Harper away from the glass.

"Yes, sweetie?"

"Cookies?" Zoey had the look on her face that Harper knew was a dead imitation of her when she was reminding Zoey of something she'd forgotten... mostly brushing her teeth. She chuckled.

"Yes, yes. I've got a tube of cookie dough in the fridge. Wash your hands, kiddo."

Harper's parents came to visit that evening, and brought her car back from Blessings Bridal—for which she was incredibly grateful. It was a relief to have her parents here to distract her from worrying all evening. They had pizza—an easy solution that reminded Harper of happier days when the Kemps would all be together on a brisk fall evening like this one.

While Harper and her father discussed the situation, Harper's mother, Grandma Georgia to Zoey, played games with her granddaughter on the living room floor.

"But they didn't get into the store," her father was saying, keeping his voice low. "Something must have scared them off."

"True," Harper agreed. "But no one noticed, either!"

"Neighbors aren't what they used to be," her father said with a shake of his head. "Used to be, you could count on the entire street to snoop into your business! A loud sneeze would get everyone's attention."

Harper chuckled at the imagery. "Well, once this is taken care of, we're going to upgrade the security system and hire more staff so that no one works alone."

Her father nodded. "And what about Gabe? How is he doing with—you know?"

She did know. "He said that he's decided to go back to the city and be a more distanced part of Zoey's life."

Her father raised his eyebrows, but remained silent.

"I don't think that's a bad thing, Dad. We were afraid he'd try to take custody of her, so considering that he's willing to leave well enough alone—"

"It's easier for you," her father replied.

"This isn't about me, and I know it." She sighed. "It's about Zoey. But fatherhood was a big shock. He never planned on having kids. He has a lot of issues to sort through, and he doesn't want to be a hands-on father."

"He's missing out," her father said sadly.

It wasn't just Gabe who was missing out, but Zoey, too. Harper had seen Gabe and Zoey playing together in the leaves, and they'd started to bond. Not only that, Gabe wasn't quite as bad with kids as he seemed to think. He'd been every bit the dad that afternoon—right down to the protective streak when it came to Zoey's safety. But Harper's heart was heavy, too…

"As a man, it's hard to process becoming a father—even when you planned it," her father said quietly. "Fatherhood is a different beast. In every other role in your life, you're expected to be tough, strong, rugged…but being a dad puts that on its head. You've got to be tender, gentle, quiet…you have to nurture. It's hard to switch gears."

"Especially with little girls," Harper agreed.

"Oh, that's for sure. I tried to get all rough and tumble with you exactly once. You screamed at me, cried and stomped off to your mother. I felt like a monster."

Harper chuckled. "You're an amazing dad."

"I grew into it. Gabe hasn't had the chance to grow into having a four-year-old daughter."

Harper still couldn't forget the sadness in Gabe's eyes when he drove away that afternoon. Such deep, murky emotion.

"He seems…sad," Harper confessed.

"He's planning on walking away from his little girl. That's bound to break a heart—even if he pretends it doesn't."

"He's trying to protect Zoey and me, but I'm worried about him, Dad."

"Feeling sorry for the guy, are you?" Her father smiled ruefully. "That's a new one. You've never been a fan of Gabe Banks."

"I was never a fan of Andrea lying to him, either," Harper retorted.

"I know, I know… Has he turned out to be human, after all?"

"It appears so." She sighed, her gaze moving toward the doorway that led to the living room. Zoey's laughter filtered into the kitchen—fueled by cookies and the bag of chips her parents brought along with him. Zoey was loved, but would they be enough for her? A father—a real dad—he'd be incredibly hard to replace.

"You'll be co-parenting with him for the rest of your

life," her father said thoughtfully. "It's good he's turned out to be human."

"He has no one to talk to," Harper said after a moment.

"Oh, that can't be true," her father replied.

"I'm not joking, Dad. He doesn't have any support here. He's keeping to himself. He only ever had his grandma here, and she's gone, so..."

His grandmother was also a different person than any of them suspected. But that wasn't her tale to tell.

"He has you, Harper."

She looked over at her father in surprise.

"You're raising a child together—and whatever that balance is going to be, you'll be in each other's lives for the next...forever." Her father heaved a sigh. "Harper, I've never raised a child with someone I wasn't in love with, but that act of child rearing with another person— it's beyond friendship. It's like an ally in battle. You're in the trenches together. You're making plans, trying to out-think this little person you're responsible for. Love or not—that's a relationship. And you'll be a support for each other that no one else can be."

Gabe wasn't quite as alone as he imagined—her dad was right about that. And if he needed someone to help him through the shock of this, who was better than her—the one raising his daughter?

"What would you think about babysitting tonight?" Harper asked.

"You going to go check on him?" her father asked.

"Someone has to." She smiled ruefully. "You're right. He and I are going to be allies, at the very least. We're Zoey's parents. So we'd better start acting like it."

"Your mother and I would be glad to spoil our granddaughter rotten." Her father smiled indulgently. "Do what you have to do, Harper. We've got your back."

Gabe could hear the toddler crying through the floor-boards. Bryce was downstairs in the kitchen—Gabe knew that much. And little Emily was howling. Outside, the sun had set, and Gabe had come upstairs to his bedroom to read. Normally, Bryce and Lily stayed in the guesthouse, but for whatever reason, the toddler seemed to be in the main house today.

Gabe rubbed his hands over his face. He couldn't think like this. Kids crying…he wasn't the kind of guy who dealt with this very well. Dads seemed to roll with it. Him? His head was pounding.

"I've got to get out of here," he muttered to himself, tossing his Bible onto his bed and grabbing his jacket off the back of a chair. He'd get a coffee, or just drive. Anything was better than this.

As Gabe came down the staircase, the crying came toward him, and he found himself face-to-face with Bryce.

"Hi," Gabe said awkwardly.

"Sorry, this isn't ideal," Bryce said with a wince. "I'm going to start dinner, and she's got an upset tummy. Don't you, Emily?"

Emily's cries stopped for a moment, and she hic-cuped. Then the tears started once more, and Bryce adjusted the little girl in his arms. He seemed so natural, as if a howling toddler was no big deal.

"Where's Lily?" Gabe asked.

"She took her little brothers to a movie," Bryce replied. "So I'm manning the fort."

"And left you to babysit?" Gabe asked with an awkward laugh.

"This isn't babysitting," Bryce replied. "This is parenting."

As if on cue, Emily promptly vomited all over the floor. Gabe closed his eyes for a moment, grossed out.

"And this—" He felt a small, warm body thrust into his arms "—*is* babysitting. Thanks, man. Just hold her for a couple of minutes while I wipe up the mess."

And Gabe was paying good money for this pleasure. He squinted down into the toddler's face and she smiled weakly.

"Feel better now?" Gabe asked dryly.

The little girl leaned her head against his shoulder and sighed.

"You aren't upset to be left on your own with the sick kid?" Gabe asked as Bryce came back into the room with a spray bottle, a bucket and a cloth.

"Nah." Bryce put down the bucket and wrung out the cloth. "A hundred good days don't add up to one bad day."

"What does that mean?"

"I mean, at the end of the day, holding her when she's sick means a whole lot more than pushing her on a swing. It's about the bonding. The hard days give you way more points than the good days do. In a little girl's heart, at least."

Those words stung. He'd be leaving all those hard days for Harper.

"You get better at it," Bryce said, spraying some disinfectant onto the freshly wiped floor. "Don't look so spooked."

"Yeah, right." Gabe tried to smile. He wasn't going to

get better at it. He was going to back out and let Harper continue with her plans. For the most part, at least.

There was a knock at the front door, and Bryce went to open it. Gabe looked down at Emily's flushed little face, and he wondered what Zoey had been like at this age. It would have been Andrea holding her when she was sick…and maybe Harper would have lent a hand sometimes. But he hadn't even known that she existed… or that there was a point system where he was severely behind.

"Hi, Harper," Bryce said. "Come on in."

Harper? Gabe looked up in guilty surprise. Where the guilt came from he wasn't even sure, until he realized he was standing here holding someone else's daughter.

"I'll be back in a second," Bryce said, heading back to the kitchen with his cleaning supplies.

Gabe eyed Harper for a second. "I thought you were staying in?"

"Changed my mind." She shrugged. "Looks like you made a friend."

Gabe looked down at the little girl in his arms. "I'm, uh, just holding her until all the vomit is cleaned up."

Harper laughed softly. "Oh, a sick tummy?" She reached out and touched Emily's cheek. "Poor girl."

Bryce returned to the foyer and scooped his daughter out of Gabe's arms. "Thanks, man. Carry on with whatever you were going to do. Much appreciated."

And without another word, Bryce headed back into the kitchen, talking softly to his daughter about having her first taste of ginger ale, and wondering if Mommy would have a good reason against it.

Gabe looked over at Harper helplessly. "That was intense."

"That?" Harper shook her head. "It's vomit. You'll see a lot of that." Then she stopped, her smile slipping. "Or not. I just meant—"

"Kids. Yeah, I get it." He sighed. This wasn't helping. He didn't need more reminders about how he was failing. He was pretty clear about that part. It was like his grandmother's voice drilling into his skull all over again. He was a walking, breathing disappointment to women countywide.

"What do you need?" he asked. She'd come here for a reason.

"Oh…I just—" Harper's cheeks tinged pink. "I was worried about you."

"Me? You're the one defying police orders."

She chuckled. "Yeah, yeah. But my dad pointed out that having paternity sprung on a guy can be a pretty intense experience. And I'm your partner in this—we're Zoey's parents. So I thought I'd come in a gesture of—"

"Defiance of a police officer's solid advice?" He couldn't help the teasing smile that twitched at the corner of his lips.

"Friendship." She smiled weakly. "We're in this together, Gabe. However we sort it all out—it's you and me. We're the adults in the situation. And if we do this right, we'll always be able to rely on each other."

"Starting now, I take it?" he asked, trying not to sound quite as bitter as he felt.

"That was the thought." Her lips parted as if to say something more, and then she pressed them shut. Her hair was pulled away from her face making her look softer, somehow more open. She was right—he could use a friend about now. He glanced back toward the kitchen. Bryce was busy with his daughter. Parenting—he'd been set straight on that one.

"You want to go outside and talk?" he asked after a beat of silence.

"I really do." She smiled gratefully, and Gabe nodded toward the door.

"After you," he said, reaching for the doorknob and pulling the door open.

They went outside together and Gabe pulled the door solidly shut behind him, grateful for the silence of a small-town night. And fresh air. After Emily's up-chuck, he was just glad to smell leaves and soil. They headed over to a hanging swing on the porch, and he waited until she'd sat down before he joined her. The rocking was oddly comforting, and the cool night felt good against his skin. Harper's shoulder pressed gently against his, and he had to stop himself from sliding his arm around her. That would be too much.

"Are you okay, Gabe?" Harper asked quietly.

He was mildly surprised at the question. He was expecting her to want to hash out parenting plans of some sort. Nail it down.

"Uh—" He shrugged weakly. "Yeah."

She looked over at him, green eyes searching his face.

"No," he admitted. "I'm feeling like a jerk for leaving in a few days."

"You have job," she said simply.

"But I'm walking away from my kid. I don't think that makes me much of a dad. Bryce in there—he's a dad. Look at him. He was mopping up puke, laughing it off, and chitchatting with a toddler…"

"He's a good dad," Harper agreed. "But every father is different. There isn't one type of dad. Some are more playful than others. Some are more serious. My father never played with me on the floor. If I wanted his attention, I'd sit with him at the table, and I'd color a picture while he read the paper, and we'd talk. I loved it."

"I didn't have a father," he said simply. There were no memories. Just a black hole where he'd been struggling to gain a foothold with his unpredictable grandmother. "I'm pretty sure that Zoey won't grow up with many fond memories of me. Her memories will be with you." He looked over at her, waiting to see how she'd react.

"Do you want that?" she asked.

"I don't know anymore," he admitted. "I…" How could he even sort his feelings on this? "I don't want her to feel unloved like I did."

"She's very loved." Tears rose in Harper's eyes. "She has me, two sets of grandparents, aunts and uncles, cousins…you."

He leaned his elbows forward onto his knees, stopping the rocking. He felt Harper's hand rest on his back.

"No one can change that you're her father," she said quietly. "I don't know if that helps, but… That's yours. And you'll figure out how to relate to her."

He nodded. Her touch was warm through his light jacket, and he found himself wanting more than this brief connection—to hold her fingers in his, to tug her closer against his side. As if that would help matters. That was old habits dying hard—looking for love in the wrong places.

He moved away from her touch. "Don't."

"Oh…" Her hand fell away, and she stood up and took a step away from him.

"It's just—" He met her gaze solemnly. "I might not be much of one, Harper, but I'm still a man."

She nodded, then licked her lips. "I'm sorry. I'm still trying to sort this out, too. How to raise my daughter with someone who—" She didn't finish the phrase, but he knew what she meant. Someone who wasn't her romantic partner. Yeah, him, too.

"I thought it would make raising Zoey together easier," he said with a sad smile.

"Maybe it will." She sucked in a deep breath. "I'm not pressuring you for anything, Gabe." But her voice trembled slightly as she said it.

Gabe rose to his feet and crossed the porch in three long strides. He wrapped his arms around her and pulled her solidly into his chest. Harper stiffened in surprise, then after a moment, rested her cheek against his shoulder and exhaled a slow breath.

"I'm pretty sure this is wildly inappropriate," he murmured against her hair.

"Yup," she agreed quietly.

"I don't know how to do this with you," he whispered. "I don't know how to stay away from you and open up at the same time." She didn't answer, and he rested his cheek against her soft curls. "But I promised God that I wouldn't play games with a woman again. I wouldn't lead her on."

Harper pulled back and looked up into his face. "You aren't leading me on, Gabe."

Yeah, well he sure would be if he did what every cell in his body wanted him to do right now, and kiss her. Her dewy eyes searched his, and he wished he could hide his feelings from her. Her lips looked so soft in the moonlight, and he had to physically hold himself back from dipping his head down and catching those lips with his.

"If you ever just want to talk," Harper said, "I'm here. You've got my number."

"Thanks. Same here."

Harper dropped her gaze. "I shouldn't have come tonight."

But he was glad she did. Whatever was stewing between them was downright dangerous, and he wished that a life of faith made it easier to just turn it off. But God wasn't answering that prayer. Why, he had no idea. How was this good for either of them?

"Harper, it's late." He took a step back. It was late, the night was beautiful, and the moonlight was reflecting off her luminous eyes in a way that was making everything spin. She needed to leave, and he needed to pull himself together.

"Oh." She nodded quickly. "Yeah, I'll head home. I didn't mean to disturb you—"

"You didn't," he said quickly. "It isn't you, Harper. It's me. I'm still a man, and you're a beautiful woman. I know my own weaknesses here." Especially when it came to her.

Harper pulled her keys from her pocket. "I know this isn't helpful," she said softly. "But I missed you."

Gabe stared at her in agony. She wasn't making this any easier! "Me, too."

"I'll see you tomorrow." She took another step away. "Dad is going to man the shop during the day, and I'm going to be going through résumés. I need to hire some help—after this is wrapped up, of course."

"Okay. Sounds good."

She wouldn't need him for more than patrol. That's

what he was hearing between the lines, and while it was strangely painful to hear, he was glad of it. He could use a day or two of getting his head on straight while he circled these streets.

"Good night, Gabe."

He raised his hand in a small wave as she went back down the front steps and headed for her car.

Why did he have to still feel like this when it came to Harper Kemp? He'd chalked the intensity of those teenage feelings up to adolescence, but it hadn't changed. She could still make his palms sweat, and his breath stick in his throat. She left him feeling off balance and wishing he could be more to her... And he was still no good for her—for *them*.

The responsible thing to do—the manly thing—was to step away. He'd promised God not to toy with a woman's emotions again, and that was a vow he would not break.

Chapter Thirteen

"So..." The chief moved his mug of coffee squarely in front of him, then met Gabe's gaze evenly. "How was the notebook?"

It was time to review his progress this week, and Gabe was now seriously wishing he hadn't written half as much as he had. The notebook had been grudgingly useful, but it was private, too.

"I used it," he said, putting it on the desk in front of him. "And it wasn't easy."

"Good." The chief didn't reach for the notebook, but instead took a sip of coffee. "It wasn't meant to be easy. It was meant to replace the binders."

"Yeah." Gabe nodded. "Right."

"And what did you learn about yourself?" The chief still hadn't reached for the little notebook, and Gabe eyed it protectively.

"Are you going to read it?" Gabe asked tentatively.

"If you want me to," the chief said with a shrug. "I'm assuming it's pretty personal, though."

"Yeah." Gabe heaved a sigh of relief and pulled the notebook back into his lap. "It is."

"So what did you learn?" Chief Morgan repeated.

"That I was a real piece of work when I lived here." He smiled bitterly. And he didn't blame Harper one bit for steering clear of him...or for encouraging Andrea to do the same. "I was a bully. I broke the law—but didn't get caught. I was a player. I was looking for something that I didn't even know I was missing."

"What's that?" the chief asked.

Gabe opened his mouth to respond, then thought twice. His answer wasn't going to be PC, and wasn't that part of sensitivity training—steering clear of inappropriate topics?

"Go ahead. Just spit it out," the chief said.

"I was missing God." Gabe winced. "I know I'm not supposed to talk about that here. We're in a professional setting and all that, but it's the truth. I was raised in church, but I never did embrace Jesus. Not until a few years ago, and my faith has changed a whole lot."

The chief nodded slowly. "But you're here. Being disciplined."

Gabe deserved that judgment. He was a Christian, and he was supposed to be better than this. And he was better than he'd been before. He'd learned a lot. God had shown him boundaries—how to draw a line and stick to it. It was turning out to be harder with Harper than it was with anyone else, but that didn't mean he couldn't do it.

"I didn't say I was fixed." Gabe smiled blandly. "I'm better than I was, and I'll keep growing in the right direction."

"What makes you so sure?"

"I'm going back to Fort Collins. I need the space from this town. Coming back here has stirred up a lot of old memories, but I'm not staying here, am I? I'm going back to my life, my precinct…and I'll behave myself this time around. No more mouthing off."

The chief was silent. Unconvinced, maybe? Gabe wasn't sure. What was the chief looking for?

"I know where my problems with authority stem from," Gabe added.

"Where?"

Gabe licked his lips. "My grandmother. I've been fighting her every day of my life. Even now."

"Why?" the chief asked.

"She didn't love me."

The chief raised his eyebrows. "Really?"

"Believe what you want about her, Chief, but she resented having to raise me. I was a burden, and she made sure I knew it."

"Ah. Now, that's some insight."

"Deep enough to let me out of here?" Gabe asked with a wry smile.

The chief was silent for a moment, then nodded. "You have a few more days of patrol, and we're still trying to crack that Blessings Bridal robbery. But if you keep your nose clean until then, I'll sign off on your training."

"Thanks, sir," Gabe said. "I appreciate that."

"I'm a Christian, too," the chief said quietly. "And you're right. We aren't supposed to be talking religion here at work, but faith does make a difference. A big one. Doesn't make it less work, but… He gives us strength."

The men regarded each other in silence for a couple of beats, and then the chief gave him a nod. "Dismissed, Officer Banks."

Gabe rose. This stay in Comfort Creek was the most challenging two weeks of his life. And here he was hoping he'd be a better man for it, because he'd learned one thing: he'd better find a way to make some peace with his grandmother's memory, or he'd never be any kind of father for his daughter. Staying away completely wasn't the answer—she'd only wonder why her dad didn't love her. He'd have to find a balance that let him keep his own life, but have a foot in his daughter's life, too.

Zoey couldn't grow up like he had—wondering what made him fundamentally unlovable. So Gabe had some work to do of his own. Ultimately, that would mean being able to let another man be "daddy."

He didn't like to think about that part—of another man holding Harper close, picking up Zoey from daycare, being with them in the evenings and calling them his—but that was the logical outcome, wasn't it? Another man would do the job that he couldn't.

Harper's father manned the store as they'd planned, and Harper went over some résumés, then spent the rest of the day with her daughter. They read together— Harper was reading her the full-length *Winnie-the-Pooh* novels, and while Zoey didn't understand all the British humor, she would lean against Harper's arm and listen to the tender, melodic story about a bear who might not have been very smart, but who was an excellent friend.

The day passed quickly enough, and that evening, Harper called Andrea's mom and asked if she'd come babysit.

"I left some wedding dresses in the back room," she explained. "And while I'm there, there are a few things

I need to get done. I don't want Zoey near the store right now—not with everything going on."

"That's why Zoey has grandparents," Jane reassured her. "I'll be over in a few minutes. Don't worry about bath time or jammies. I'll take care of everything."

Harper could have hugged the woman through the phone. "Thank you!"

"You aren't going there alone, are you?" Jane asked.

"No, I'll let Gabe know I'm dropping by. He can meet me there."

Jane was satisfied and within fifteen minutes she'd arrived with a smile and a hug for her granddaughter.

"I'm just going to the store," Harper explained to Zoey. She bent and pressed a kiss against her daughter's forehead. "Be good for Grandma?"

"I'm always good," Zoey said innocently. "Grandma needs to watch my unicorn show. She misses it."

Harper chuckled and hitched her purse up on her shoulder. "Thanks, Jane. I won't be too long."

Harper got into her car, and she was on her way to the store before she voice-dialed Gabe on her cell phone. He picked up on the third ring.

"Harper? Everything okay?" He sounded alarmed.

"Everything's fine," she said. "I'm stopping by the store to pick up a few things. It won't take me more than ten minutes. Just thought I should let you know."

"Yeah, you should definitely let me know!" There was a rustling sound. "I'm on my way. Where are you now?"

"Around the corner from the store," she said, signaling her turn. "You don't need to—"

"Yes, I do," he snapped. "I'm on my way."

There were a few more mutters of annoyance, and

then he hung up. She sighed. Harper parked behind the store in her usual spot, and she saw a police cruiser pass on the street next to her at a reassuringly slow pace.

"It'll be fine," she said aloud. And it would be—she couldn't be scared away from her store—this was *her* life! Blessings Bridal and Blessings Maternity…these stores would be her legacy, and one day when Zoey was older, she'd be able to appreciate what her mom had built. Maybe Zoey would add to it with her own store. Blessings Kids? Blessings Toys? Harper grinned to herself. The possibilities were endless, and that's what she liked about growing a business.

Harper got out of the car and locked it, then headed around to the front door. She paused, looking up and down the street—waiting for Gabe. Then she looked in the window, glanced at her watch and wondered if it would be so terrible to just go in quickly and grab those dresses. She wouldn't stop and do anything else. The street was quiet, and the soft rustle of leaves shifting in the breeze was comforting. Maybe these criminals had seen how quickly the police responded and had changed their minds about another return to Comfort Creek, after all.

Harper unlocked the front door and let herself in. She pulled it shut behind her and slid the lock into place. Then she typed the code into the security system and headed for the back room.

Harper flicked the switch in the back room, the overhead globe shedding soft light. Harper headed for the two boxed wedding dresses, stretching onto her tiptoes to reach them down from a shelf.

Outside, she heard a clank, and she looked up. Could that be right? She lifted her head and listened. From the front of the store, she heard a shuffle, another clanking sound. Her heart leaped to her throat, and Harper tried to swallow, but couldn't.

It was probably Gabe…except she'd locked up behind her. She pulled out her cell phone and looked down at it. No missed texts.

"Gabe?" she called, but her voice sounded strangled, and it didn't go very far. That wasn't Gabe—she could feel it in her gut.

There was another shuffling sound, then a thump. She wasn't going out there. If she startled robbers, who knew what might happen? She dialed Gabe's number and lifted her phone to her ear, just as she heard the crash of breaking glass.

"Harper? I'm almost there."

"Someone's in here," she whispered into the phone.

"Can you get out?" he asked briskly, and she heard a siren go on through the phone.

Harper looked around to the back door. "I can, but the bolt is noisy. If I push it, they'll hear."

There would be no creeping out of the store—that was for sure. If she made a run for it, they'd know!

"I want you to find a place to hide and stay low. Don't say anything else, but stay on the line with me, okay?"

Harper crept into a back corner and crouched down. The light still blazed from above, and she wished she could flick it off, but if she did, she'd only call more attention to herself. Her hands trembled and she tried to control her breathing, but it sounded loud in her own ears. More thumping and a scrape from the sales floor, and Harper squeezed her eyes shut, sending up a prayer for safety.

What had she been thinking, coming inside alone?

She should have just cooperated with Gabe—this had been foolhardy.

Lord, protect me!

"Police!" a voice roared, and there was the sound of scrambling in the other room. There was a shout, and then the *pop-pop* of a gun firing. Harper sank lower to the floor, putting her hands over her head.

"Go, go, go!" another voice shouted, then it lowered into a professional tone. "We have three perps fleeing on foot heading north through the alley behind Main Street and Hudson. We need to cut them off."

She knew that voice—it was Gabe, and he wasn't alone. He'd come with backup. She almost sobbed with relief when his form darkened the doorway.

"Harper!" he barked, and she slid out of her hiding place, tears welling in her eyes.

Gabe didn't say another word—he just strode across the room and gathered her up into his arms. He held her so close that her ribs ached under the pressure, but she didn't care. He'd come just in time, and her heart was pounding hard in her chest. Seeing Gabe had flooded her heart with more emotion than she thought possible.

"You okay?" Gabe asked gruffly, pulling back to look at her.

"Just a scare," she said with a shaky smile. "I'm glad you're here."

"You shouldn't have come inside without me—" He stopped, closed his eyes. "But you know that. For crying out loud, Harper, if anything happened to you!"

"Quit yelling at me," she said with a shaky smile.

He pushed her curls out of her face and cupped her cheeks in his hands. Then he lowered his lips, exhaling his own deep sigh as his mouth covered hers in a long kiss. His hand moved from her face to pull her close against his broad chest once more, and she sank into that embrace. She felt like she belonged there—right next to his beating heart.

"Officer Banks, have you secured the civilian?" a voice crackled over his radio, and Gabe released her with a rueful smile.

"Affirmative," he said into the radio. "She's fine." Then he dialed down the volume on his radio to leave them undisturbed. "The other officers will be chasing down the robbers. We had them in our sights."

Harper nodded. "So it's going to be over... I won't have to worry."

Harper leaned back into his arms and he rested his cheek on her hair.

"That was stupid to come in without waiting for me." His voice had lowered to a growl, but his grip as he held her didn't loosen. "I'm trying to keep you safe. If something had happened to you—for crying out loud, I love you!"

Harper pulled back and stared up at him. "What?"

"Is that crazy?" He stared down at her miserably. "I'm in love with you, Harper. This isn't just a crush or me wanting to take out the bad guy. I've been around long enough to know I've never felt this with any other woman before...and I tried not to feel it with you...I really did. I did everything I could to keep from falling for you, but when you sounded so scared, I couldn't deny it anymore. I'm head over heels in love with you. Whatever that's worth."

Harper's heart hammered in her throat, and she felt her eyes welling with tears. "I love you, too."

"Yeah?" A smile tugged at one side of his mouth.

"Not that it matters...does it?" she whispered miserably.

"Matters to me," he replied gruffly.

"But you don't want this, Gabe," she whispered. "This life—kids, a wife. And I can't just hang on the line for you, loving you and knowing that we can never pull together and be husband and wife properly. You don't want the package—"

"I want *you*," he replied fiercely.

"I come with Zoey. I'm setting up a new business here in Comfort Creek. My family is here, my life is here..."

Gabe released her and scrubbed a hand through his tousled curls.

"Unless you've changed your mind about being a family?" she asked hopefully.

His answer was in the misery in his eyes. He shook his head slowly. "I promised God I wouldn't jerk another woman around, and look at me. I shouldn't have told you how I felt."

"Of course, you should have!" she shot back, but sadness lowered onto Harper's chest. "We both tried not to feel this, Gabe..."

He reached forward to touch her cheek gently. "I love you more than I thought was even possible for a man to feel... But love isn't enough—"

This wasn't Gabe's fault; Harper couldn't blame him. They'd both known this from the start. Loving each other wasn't enough to make a life together. But respect might be enough to parent the little girl they both loved.

"What do we do?" Gabe asked at last, that dark gaze moving over her face searchingly, as if she held the answer somehow. But Harper wasn't holding on to some secret wisdom. She was as lost as he was.

"We get over this," Harper said woodenly, forcing the words out. "We go our separate ways, we lick our wounds, and we...get over it. For Zoey's sake."

"For Zoey..."

Footsteps could be heard outside, and Bryce appeared in the doorway.

"They've apprehended the perps—" Bryce stopped short. "Am I interrupting?"

"No," Gabe said quickly, then he cleared his throat. "Glad to hear it. I've got a personal interest in these guys, so I'm going to go down to the station for their statements. You think you could see Miss Kemp home for me?"

Bryce nodded, glancing between the two of them. "Sure thing. Are you okay, Harper? You look pretty shaken up."

Gabe looked over at Harper once last time, and he blinked back a mist in his eyes. "I'll come back to say goodbye to Zoey. And then I'll go home."

Harper's heart sank—this was it. He'd be going back to his life in the city, and she'd be the heartbroken wreck left behind. For all her warnings to her best friend, Harper hadn't done any better. She'd lost her heart to this man against her better judgment.

"I'll be in touch, though," Gabe added.

Harper nodded, tears welling in her eyes. Not in front of the other cop! She didn't want to cry—that was for later, when she was alone and she could vent this grief inside of her. Gabe strode from the room, and it took all of Harper's strength not to run after him. Hot tears seared a trail down her cheeks.

"It's been a rough night," Bryce said, putting a hand on her elbow and handing over her coat. "Let me get you home, Harper. Some tea and a hug from your little girl will set you right. I can call your parents, if you want..."

Harper picked up her purse and allowed herself to be led from the room and through her store. The robbers hadn't had the chance to do much damage, but there was a gown on the floor, trampled by muddy boots. And a rack of dresses had pitched onto one side.

Bryce talked to her the whole time, but she'd tuned him out. Gabe was gone, and when Bryce opened the car door for her, she realized that she didn't even remember getting outside. She shivered, rubbing her hands together.

"It's a blessing you weren't hurt," Bryce said as she sank into the warm depths of the police cruiser.

A blessing. So many blessings. And not one of them was the ability to be with the man she loved.

Chapter Fourteen

That night, Harper lay in bed and sobbed out her grief. Falling in love with Gabe had been a bad idea from the start, and she'd done her best to keep her emotions in check. When her tears were spent, she lay on her back, staring up at the ceiling.

*Father, You've blessed me...*she prayed silently. *I have family, a daughter of my own, a chance to start a second store in the town where I was born. You've blessed me abundantly, and still my heart is broken. I love him, Lord. I do. I shouldn't—I tried not to! But I love him, and I miss him already.*

Fresh tears welled in her eyes. *But I still trust You. I am still Yours. And if Gabe is not the man for me, then I leave my heart in Your hands to heal and make whole again.*

That was when she felt a warmth wrap around her and her eyes grew heavy. She hadn't thought she'd sleep tonight, but after a moment or two, she closed her eyes. It would hurt—there was no getting around that—but God still had a plan for her. Maybe her life would never be traditional, but it would be meaningful. Maybe God had simply shown her that Gabe was a good man so that she could work together with him to raise Zoey. Maybe this hadn't been about her, at all, and this was God working things out for her daughter's best interest.

An image of Gabe rose up in her mind—strong, muscular, steel gray eyes pinning her to the spot. He'd been easier to fall for than she'd imagined. But it hadn't changed anything—Gabe wasn't a family man. And it wasn't his fault, either.

Where was Gabe now? Maybe he was still working, tying up the loose ends of his case against these criminals. She could imagine him at a desk in the police station, angrily pounding out a report or two, and the thought made her smile. Or maybe he'd be back at the Camden bed and breakfast already, lying in his own bed, praying for his own peace.

Harper didn't remember when, but her thoughts were overcome by a wave of tiredness and she fell into a fitful sleep.

She awoke the next morning to small hands tugging on her blanket, and Harper felt tired and dehydrated. She moaned.

"What time is it, Zoey?"

"Time for breakfast," Zoey said. "Are you awake yet, Mommy? Maybe a little bit?"

Harper couldn't help but smile. "A little bit," she confirmed, and scooted over to make room for her daughter in her bed. She patted the mattress next to her, and Zoey squirmed up and wriggled under the covers.

"How did you sleep?" Harper murmured, rubbing her eyes. It was Saturday morning, and they had a routine together, which started with snuggles in "the big bed."

"Good." Zoey reached over and touched Harper's face. "Did you cry, Mommy?"

Was it still so evident? Harper sighed. "Yes, sweetie. But I'm better now."

"Sometimes I cry when I miss Mommy." Andrea. She was talking about missing Andrea.

Harper's eyes misted in spite of herself. "And it's okay to cry when we miss people. Just make sure you come for hugs when you do, okay?"

Morning sunlight sparkled on a frost-laden lawn out the window, and Harper sent up a silent prayer of gratefulness. No one had everything, but she had Zoey, and Zoey was gift enough.

The phone rang from the bedside table, and Harper stretched to grab it, picking it up on the second ring. She recognized the number—her sister's.

"Hi, Heidi," Harper said, scooting up in bed to be able to sit up.

"Harper —I heard about the store! Are you okay? What happened? Did you see them?"

"Hold on." Harper looked over at her daughter. Zoey's eyes were pinned on her. "One second, Heidi." Harper covered the mouthpiece. "Zoey, I'm going to let you have a juice box this morning."

"Really?" Zoey looked impressed. "Those are for lunches."

"Just once. A special treat. If you go and get it right now."

Zoey didn't need to be asked twice, and launched off the bed and out the door, her bare feet slapping against the hardwood floor as she careened toward the kitchen.

The next few minutes were spent filling her sister in on the latest break-in and the arrest of the robbers.

Harper kept the part about her and Gabe to herself, though. That was private. She wasn't sure she'd ever talk about it—not in full detail. She and Gabe might not be a match romantically, but the secrets he'd shared were still safe with her.

When she'd finished answering all her sister's questions, they both fell silent for a moment.

"I have news…" Heidi's voice quivered just a little.

"Oh, no… What's the matter?" she asked.

"There won't be a wedding." There were tears in Heidi's voice, and Harper felt a wave of pity. This was what she'd been afraid of—Heidi dumping yet another good guy. Why did she keep doing this?

"What happened?" Harper asked.

"I talked to Chris about lying to him…and we talked and talked and talked." Heidi was silent for a moment. "In the end, he broke it off."

"Him?" Harper gasped.

"Yeah. He said he wants more. He loves me, and he thought that commitment would make us closer, but…" Heidi's voice trailed off. "He did it for me. I might have just gone through with it. I've broken too many hearts and the wedding plans had already gone so far… But as it turns out, he couldn't go through with it."

"Heidi, I'm so sorry," Harper breathed. "I'm not in great shape this morning, either."

"What's going on? Is it Gabe?" Heidi asked.

"How did you know?"

"You aren't as secretive as you think," her sister replied. "So what happened between you two?"

"It's a long story. We were getting to know each other, and he's not the man I thought. Not anymore, at least. I don't think he opens up to many people, but he did with me, and I could see the man he is deep down, under that tough-guy act he has going on all the time..."

"So he won you over?" Heidi asked.

"He said he loves me."

"You poor dear," her sister said flatly. "My heart bleeds for you."

The very thing Harper had told her own sister a few days ago.

"Very funny. It won't work, Heidi," Harper said. "He can't be a family man, and I have Zoey. It's just—not meant to be. Feelings aren't enough—they don't change reality."

"But you love him, too?" Heidi asked.

"Yeah." Harper's throat tightened, and she swallowed hard. "More than anything."

The sisters were silent for a few beats, and then Heidi said, "I made you cut the dress."

"It's okay," Harper said.

"I feel terrible about that," Heidi said. "Grandma's dress—it was an heirloom, Harper! I'm so selfish!"

"Look, it's okay," Harper said. "Maybe it's even for the best in some twisted way. I had this image in my mind of the perfect life I wanted. My husband would be educated, well read, smart and a little athletic. He'd have it all together. I'd have three children, eighteen months apart each. I'd keep them home until kinder-garten, and I'd have that white picket fence."

"Nothing wrong with all that," Heidi said.

"It's not real, Heidi," Harper replied. "It's imaginary. And I wanted to start that perfect life by getting married in Grandma's dress. So if Grandma's dress will never be the same, maybe it's for the best. Because I don't need perfect, I just need the man I love."

"Gabe," her sister confirmed.

Her heart clenched hearing his name, and she wished that he could be part of her imperfect adventure. But he couldn't.

"Not Gabe. Because while I could accept him, flaws and all, he doesn't want a family. And not only do I have Zoey, but I'd really like a baby of my own one day. But if he'd been able to see himself as a dad, I would have been able to let my fantasy life go. I wouldn't have held him to that. Because what's a fantasy when faced with an actual life with a guy who makes your heart flutter?"

"I suppose so," Heidi agreed.

"You'll find a guy you want to be close to, Heidi," Harper added. "You will."

"I don't know what I'm going to do with myself right now," Heidi admitted. "I quit my job for the wedding…"

"I know you probably don't want to work with wedding dresses," Harper said. "But I'm going to need a manager for my new maternity shop."

"Wait—it's happening?" Heidi said.

"I just got the loan finalized. What do you say? We Kemp girls will pull together and build an empire."

"I always thought I'd marry into one," Heidi said, but there was a smile in her voice. "But you're right— it might be easier to just build it ourselves."

Harper shook her head. "I always thought so."

"Thank you, Harper. I needed this."

"You also need chocolate and a shoulder to cry on," Harper said. "I know I do. Come over today. We'll show Zoey how empires start—women working together."

Maybe Harper's business would be good for more than just Zoey—maybe Heidi could get a glimpse of what was possible for her, too. Life seldom turned out as expected, but that didn't mean it wasn't perfectly in the center of God's will.

* * *

Gabe drove back to Fort Collins, his heart heavy. He'd expected to be exhilarated at the prospect of going home to his bachelor pad, his friends and his job…even his own church. He arrived home Saturday evening and was in his pew Sunday morning. But these last two weeks in Comfort Creek had changed everything. He was a father—that in itself was life-altering. And he'd fallen in love with a woman who wanted a family all over again.

He tried to pray about it, but God wasn't bringing the comfort he normally gave. Was this punishment for how he'd treated Andrea? He wasn't sure. But Gabe knew for a fact that he would never have God's blessing while he toyed with a woman's heart. God protected His daughters.

So Gabe went through the motions of his life in Fort Collins—working his shifts, cooking meals, heading out with friends for wings one evening… He even went to church and tried to find that peaceful sanctuary once more, but he was still left empty and aching. Why? He had done the right thing—he'd stepped back. He would not toy with another woman's feelings! He was keeping his vow to his Maker. Why wouldn't God give him some relief?

One evening, a week after he'd arrived back at home, Gabe stood in his living room holding that old, worn Bible his grandmother had left to him. It had taken him this long to take it out of the box, and looking down at it, he felt a wave of anger.

"Father, she claimed to love You," Gabe murmured. "She said she put You first in everything, but she was the coldest, hardest, cruelest woman I've ever known."

The fact that his grandmother had left him her Bible only rubbed in that ridiculous fact. Weren't Christians supposed to be known by their love? His grandmother was dead now, and Gabe honestly had no idea if she'd been saved or not. All he knew was that she'd been a church goer and a Bible reader. Was it possible to read the Bible every day and career right past the Author?

Gabe sank down onto the couch, the old Bible in his hands, and he let it fall open. The pages were brittle and a little tattered. His grandmother had been a Bible marker, and she had other verses noted down next to underlined verses. He leafed through Genesis, Exodus, Leviticus, then let it fall shut again.

"It isn't about her, Lord, it's about me," he prayed. "I'm angry. I haven't forgiven her! I needed her to love me, and she couldn't do that."

Tears welled in his eyes, and he put the Bible down.

"I'm trying so hard!" His voice cracked. It had been easier to be a jerk all those years ago. At least he'd just surfed along with his baser instincts. Now that he was trying to live a Christian life, he was fighting those instincts every step of the way.

If he stopped fighting it, he'd drive straight back to Comfort Creek and pull Harper into his arms again. That would be a powerful comfort right about now... But he'd never stay. He couldn't face that town day in and day out. He couldn't make a life in the very place where his grandmother had emotionally kicked him around. It was because of his upbringing that he wasn't emotionally prepared to be a proper father. And very likely, Zoey would grow up resenting him, too, for not being able to be the dad she needed. It was a vicious cycle.

Gabe rose to his feet and sucked in a shaky breath.

He glanced at the time on his cell phone. He wanted to call Harper, to hear her voice. He could make an excuse—say he was asking about his daughter, but he didn't want to toy with Zoey's feelings, either. She needed a life without complication, and it wasn't her job to make Gabe feel better.

Zoey had to come first. Her equilibrium mattered a far sight more than his. So he put his phone down, and his gaze moved back toward that battered Bible.

Should he keep it? Give it away to charity? Misused by its original owner or not, that was still a Bible, and he couldn't bring himself to desecrate it in any way. He bent and picked it up again.

He flipped through the pages once more, and this time stopped toward the end of the Bible in the book of James. A verse had been underlined that caught his eye: "Every good gift and every perfect gift is from above, and cometh down from the Father of lights, with whom is no variableness, neither shadow of turning." Next to it, in his grandmother's handwriting, was written his name.

Gabe paused, his heart thudding in his chest. When had she written that? Had she actually seen Gabe as a gift from God?

Did she realize it too late, after he'd already left home? Or had she simply been trying to spur herself into better behavior? And maybe his grandmother was no different than he was—ill-suited to raising a child, yet thrust into the role.

Gabe knew one thing for sure—he couldn't claim to be a Christian while holding on to spite and bitterness. He'd end up no different than his grandmother if he did that.

"Father, help me to forgive her," he prayed. "I've tried so hard, and I can't do it. I need You to do this for me. Help me to forgive my grandmother for never being enough for me..."

The box lay on the coffee table, and inside was that little Popsicle stick craft. Once upon a time, he'd loved his grandmother, and as he looked at the gobs of glue, the careful printing, that old feeling came rushing back into his heart. A long time ago, he'd loved her with all of his boyish heart, and he'd tried to earn her love in return. Well, she was beyond this earth now, and he realized in a moment that his anger at her was covering over a deeper pain.

"Grandma, I love you." He wept as tears coursed down his cheeks. "And maybe I don't need you to love me back anymore."

His grandmother had been all he had—and loving her hadn't been a weakness on his part. He'd just been a kid. Loving her still—and disliking her in equal measure—didn't make him an idiot, either. Grandma Banks had been the one with the problem. Had she done her best with her limitations? He had no idea. Maybe it no longer mattered.

But it wasn't only his conflicted love for his grandmother that tore at his heart. He'd fallen in love with Harper, and he had a little girl who needed his love, too. And he needed to learn how to give it. His heart was filled with love—aching, piercing love.

Every good gift and every perfect gift is from above.

Love was the greatest gift of all—the people God put into families. And he and Harper were a family now, albeit an unconventional one. They were tied together by a little girl who'd never asked to be born, but God in His wisdom had created her.

Harper and Zoey were the perfect gifts, and he'd been running from them because he was too broken to see it. In the midst of his pain, God had given him the gift of love so deep that he couldn't wash it out. God hadn't left him alone in his pain, after all. But he had to get past his anger and down to real hurt before he could see it. Maybe, just maybe, God had been using his aching heart to bring him back home—to give him the family he'd been running from.

He stood in the center of his living room, his heart pounding in his chest. Gabe knew what he had to do, but it was risk. A big one.

Still, if he didn't follow his heart *this* time, he'd regret it for the rest of his life. Not every fundamental instinct was a wrong one. Sometimes, it was God-ordained destiny.

Chapter Fifteen

Harper unlocked the front door to her house and Zoey scampered in ahead of her. It had been another long day at Blessings Bridal, but Heidi was pitching in to give her a hand. Heidi was heartbroken over her split up with Chris, but sisters working together seemed to be more comforting for Heidi than Harper had thought possible. It was helpful for Harper, too. She tried not to talk about Gabe, but she missed him deeply.

Harper wouldn't admit to feeling anything but tired, but she also didn't think she hid it very well.

Harper looked out the window to the empty street. Days were shorter now, and across the street she could already see the lights on in the neighbor's house. Zoey flicked on lights as she went through the living room and into the kitchen.

"Mommy, when is Daddy coming?" Zoey asked.

"He said he'd be here for supper," Harper replied.

Gabe called yesterday and asked if he could come visit. He had a day off and missed them, he said. She'd agreed, of course, but she knew it would be hard. She was still in love with the man—a detail she'd have to set aside for Zoey's sake.

"What are we having?" Zoey asked.

"I'm ordering pizza." It just seemed easier, and Zoey squealed in delight at this announcement. This girl loved a good pizza.

Besides, Harper wasn't sure she could focus on cooking right now. She'd probably just burn any meal she tried to put together. It was better to keep her wits about her so she wouldn't make a fool of herself when faced with Gabe again.

Harper sucked in a deep breath, trying to calm her nerves. She and Gabe had talked a few times since he'd left—mostly because they couldn't quite let go. And she missed his voice, his eyes, the smell of his cologne... She was always checking her phone, wondering if he'd text her, even though they'd both promised not to.

"I'm being stupid," she told herself aloud.

"What, Mommy?"

"Nothing, Zoey."

A knock on the door sent Zoey running to open it, and Harper followed a few steps behind. Zoey flung open the door to reveal Gabe standing there with a wrapped package in his hands.

"A present?" Zoey said, eyes wide.

"Say hello first, Zoey," Harper chuckled.

"Hi. Is that a present?"

Gabe chuckled and handed it to her. "Just something I thought you'd like, kiddo."

Zoey carried the box a full three feet from the door before she started tearing off the paper. Harper shot Gabe a smile, and he grinned back, the sparkle in his dark eyes making her stomach flip.

"Hi," she said quietly.

"Hey…" Gabe leaned in and kissed her cheek, his lips lingering on her skin for just a moment longer than necessary. "I missed you."

"Same." She licked her lips and turned her attention to Zoey, who'd just unwrapped a child sized tool belt, complete with a selection of tools.

"Wow, oh, wow, oh, wow!" Zoey breathed. "Tools…"

Harper smiled mistily. Gabe was catching on pretty fast to the whole dad thing. Zoey would be okay, after all.

"What do you say, Zoey?" Harper prompted.

"Thanks, Daddy!" But she didn't even look up. She was too busy sorting it all out with her nimble little fingers.

Harper looked at Gabe and found his gaze locked on her. He reached over and moved a tendril of hair out of her eyes, then shrugged sheepishly.

"I couldn't stay away," he said.

"I'm glad…" But then she stopped herself. She'd promised herself not to do this. Zoey needed a mom and a dad, not two feuding exes. Or a brokenhearted mother who was jealous every time her father dated another woman. None of that was good for Zoey.

"I'm just about to order pizza," Harper said, forcing a smile. "What kind do you like? Zoey and I normally get pepperoni, but we can be flexible for guests."

"Pepperoni's fine, but—" He reached out and caught her hand. "Hold on a second."

Harper stopped and looked up at him, waiting.

"Here's the thing, Harper. I missed you. I dreamed of you. Every single waking hour I was trying not to text or call or bother you—" He winced. "I hated this town, but I realized something while I was here."

"Oh?" she breathed.

"I'm in love with you."

"We know that," she replied with a shake of her head. "But it won't work!"

"And I realized something when I got back to Fort Collins," he went on. "A chance at happiness doesn't come every day. I've never met a woman who makes me feel like you do. I steered clear of marriage, but with you, I just want to jump in headfirst."

"I'm a mom," she reminded him.

"I know. And that's why I need to man up. I have issues, granted. My grandmother was abusive, but I've finally been able to forgive her. I loved her, for all her flaws, and loving again is hard because it risks opening up. It risks…messing up! Making mistakes. Not being the perfect dad."

Harper had no words, and she stared at him, her breath caught in her throat.

"Harper, first of all, I'm going to promise you something. I'm going to man up. I'm going to face my issues, my childhood, my relationships—all of it—and I'm going to be the man you need me to be. Both of you. I've already started facing the hard stuff, and I've cried out a lot of that pain, and you know what I found at the bottom?"

Harper shook her head.

"Love." He smiled gently. "I loved my grandma, even when she hurt me. And I love my daughter, even though I don't know her very well yet. And I'm desperately, head over heels in love with you."

"I love you, too, Gabe…"

Gabe leaned over and kissed her lips ever so gently. "Then let's take a chance—see what we can do if I transfer here to Comfort Creek."

Harper's heart skipped a beat and she stared at him in shock.

"What?" she whispered. "You don't want—"

"I *know* what I want," he replied, his tone low and deep. "I want you. I want to marry you, raise our daughter together as a family, and spend the rest of my life convincing you that you made the right choice in taking on a broken cop like me."

"You want to get married?" she asked in disbelief.

"Eventually, yeah. I'll move here," he replied. "I'll face the hard stuff and I'll make Comfort Creek the home it should have been all along. I've been running from my feelings for too long. I want all of it, Harper. I want a life together, I want to be the kind of father that my daughter needs, and I want to take the first step toward that. What do you say...are you willing to take a chance on me?"

Harper threw her arms around his neck and silenced him with a kiss. His arms twined around her waist, holding her close.

"What happened?" Zoey asked, and Harper pulled back from the kiss to look down at her daughter.

"Daddy's going to move to Comfort Creek and see a whole lot more of us," Harper said with a grin.

Gabe pulled her back in for another kiss, and then bent down to scoop up Zoey into his strong arms.

Zoey was silent and thoughtful for a moment, then asked, "Where do I live, then?"

"With me," Harper said. "But you'll get to see a whole lot more of your dad, too."

Harper leaned her head against Gabe's strong shoulder.

"Pizza?" Zoey asked. "I'm hungry."

"Tell you what," Gabe said. "Let's go out and have a special meal at a restaurant, just us three." He shot Harper a tender smile. "It'll be our first date."

Gabe put down Zoey and she ran for her shoes, and as Harper looked up at this man she'd fallen for, her heart swelled with love.

"Are you sure about this?" Harper asked softly.

"All I need is you," he replied. "I'll need you to be here for me when it's hard, and when I'm sorting through my own stuff. And I want you to tell me when I'm messing up, when I need to do things differently with Zoey. I don't know how to be a dad or even a potential husband, but I'm going to learn."

"You're doing just fine, Gabe."

"What about you?" he asked, locking his eyes on hers. "Are you sure about this? Do you need some time to think about it?"

She shook her head, tears misting her vision. "I had a list of things I wanted, and then I met you, and—"

"I didn't tick all of those items off, did I?" he asked ruefully.

"I realized that my list was ridiculous," she replied with a low laugh. "It didn't take into account what it would feel like to be in love."

He loved them, and that was more than enough. Families weren't made by experts who knew what they were doing—they were the fumbled attempts of people who loved each other enough to keep trying. When they'd been married fifty years, maybe they could count as experts then…but in the meantime, Harper was happy to toss all those expectations of perfection aside and embrace the man who filled her heart.

"Hey, guys!" Zoey stood at the door, her tool belt buckled around her waist and legs akimbo. "Are we going out, or what?"

"We're going, we're going," Harper said with a laugh.

They were starting something today—something beautiful and blessed. She could feel it. God's timing was always best, and she could feel the rest of the path opening up in front of them. They'd be a family…one step at a time.

Epilogue

On a midwinter weekend, with a fresh layer of snow blanketing the ground, Harper and Gabe got married. Reverend Blake officiated, and Heidi stood as maid of honor. Gabe had Bryce Camden stand for him, and Zoey, of course, was the flower girl.

Harper didn't wear her grandmother's dress. She was keeping that dress for Heidi, because while her sister hadn't found the right guy yet, Harper knew that she would. In faith, she'd cut that dress, and in faith, she was saving it for her sister. Instead, Harper wore her grandmother's veil and one of the beautiful ball gowns she'd been eyeing all these years—tulle and beading coming together perfectly to accentuate Harper's slim figure.

The wedding was beautiful, but Harper wouldn't remember much of it. She remembered little snapshots—like the Camdens sitting together in a pew, Lily holding her sleeping daughter in her arms…or like Sadie Morgan dancing with her husband, the chief of police, and loosening him up like no one else could. And it turned out that Sadie was expecting, after all—and she was now roundly, beautifully pregnant.

Harper's most vivid memory from her wedding day was Gabe's toast during the reception. He rose to his feet, looking so handsome and rugged in a tuxedo. The murmur of the guests faded away as everyone turned their attention to the groom.

"When I asked Harper to marry me at Christmas, I knew that wasn't going to be the end of it," he said, raising his glass. "She said yes—" he raised his glass to Harper with a wink "—and then I had to talk to her father."

The guests all laughed at that point, and Gabe shot his new father-in-law a grin. "And I'd like to thank my father-in-law, Allan Kemp, for giving not only his blessing, but a whole lot of advice, too. If I can be half the man he is, I'll have done well by his daughter. I suggested that I call him Mr. Kemp from now on, but he said I should call him Dad. I never knew my own father, and by marrying Harper I've gained more than a wife—I've gained parents. So…Dad…Mom…here's to you."

Gabe turned then to the Murphys and raised his glass again. "And I'd like to thank Mike and Jane Murphy for their support, as well. They're my daughter's grandparents, as you all probably know by now, and they needed a little more convincing."

There were more chuckles from the guests.

"A few years ago, I let you down in a big way, but you took the time to sit down with me, to listen to me, and after a couple of weeks of long talks, you gave me your forgiveness and your blessing, too. And I'm grateful for that, because this family is important to my daughter, to my wife, and to me, too. I've never had a proper family before, and I feel like God has wrapped me up into layer upon layer of family in my marriage to Harper.

"And to my little girl, Zoey." He smiled down at Zoey, who was seated next to her mother. "I'm marrying your mom, but I'm also promising that I'll do right by you, too. I didn't know I was a father until I came to Comfort Creek a few months ago, and discovering you turned my life upside down in the best way possible! You're my tool-loving princess, and I love you, kiddo. I've been called a lot of things in my life, but Daddy— that's my favorite so far!

"And Harper…" His voice cracked, and he paused for a moment until he'd regained his composure. Gabe turned to Harper and met her gaze with a look of tenderness. "I love you. Heart and soul. For the rest of my life. I don't know how to say this in front of everyone here—" He glanced toward the guests, then shrugged helplessly. "You said you'd be mine, and I'm promising you—yet again—that I'll never hurt you. I'll take care of you, listen to you, support you through anything life throws at us…and I'm also making this public promise that I'm going to be taking your advice."

There was another chuckle from the guests.

"I'm serious about that." He turned to the room of people. "So if you ask a favor and I say I'm going to talk to my wife—know who the boss is around here!"

Everyone laughed.

"I love you, Harper. Here's to you, Beautiful. And to the rest of our lives together."

Gabe bent down and kissed Harper's lips. She shut her eyes, letting his love flow around her.

"I love you, too," she whispered back.

Married—she'd wondered how it would feel to be Mrs. Harper Banks, and it felt right, perfect. In this hall filled with family and friends, she could feel the depth of their vows twining them closer and closer together.

Comfort Creek, the dullest town in Colorado, had been her home for her entire life, but it was now home in a whole new way—home with Gabe. God had been so good to her that she didn't have the words to thank Him. Her prayer was a silent lifting of her heart to her Maker—the God who'd brought her Gabe Banks. The rest of her life didn't seem like long enough, but it was a very good start!

* * * * *

*If you enjoyed this story by Patricia Johns,
pick up the other books in the*
COMFORT CREEK LAWMEN *miniseries:*

*DEPUTY DADDY
THE LAWMAN'S RUNAWAY BRIDE*

Available now from Love Inspired!

Find more great reads at www.LoveInspired.com

Dear Reader,

It's hard to wait for blessings, isn't it? We get impatient, and when we see others enjoying the blessings we pray for, it can be hard. In this book, Harper has to make her peace with the love and romance she wishes she had in her life in the face of her younger sister's wedding.

When my husband and I got engaged, we told our church family. There was a woman who was a few years older than me—a single mom. She threw her arms around me with a genuine hug, and she said, "I'm so happy for you! May God bless me, too!" That stuck with me, because she was so gracious, so lovely, so genuinely happy for the joy of others, and I thought, *I want to be like her*.

It might not be easy, but I've made it a habit now that when others reach my goals before I do to say, "I'm happy for her! May God remember me, too." Because I've learned that just because God has blessed one person, doesn't mean His plans for anyone else have diminished.

If you'd like to connect with me, you can find me on Facebook, Twitter, or on my blog, PatriciaJohnsRomance.com. I'd love to see you!

Patricia Johns

COURTING HER SECRET HEART
Prodigal Daughters • by Mary Davis

Deborah Miller lives a double life as an Amish woman—and a fashion model! But when Amos Burkholder starts helping at her family's farm, she must choose between the *Englischer* world of modeling and the Amish man she's come to love.

RUNAWAY AMISH BRIDE
Colorado Amish Courtships • by Leigh Bale

Abby Miller jumps at the opportunity to marry Jakob Fisher and start a new life. But when she arrives, she learns the widower didn't know about the arrangement. As she stays on with Jakob's family to help with his kids, can Abby still find a permanent place by his side?

REUNITED WITH THE RANCHER
Mercy Ranch • by Brenda Minton

Returning home to confront his father about the past, Carson West doesn't expect to find his childhood sweetheart living on the ranch where his father takes in wounded military veterans. But could Mercy Ranch—and Kylie Baker—be the fresh start the widowed single father's been searching for?

DRY CREEK DADDY
Dry Creek • by Janet Tronstad

Four years ago, an accident put Mark Nelson into a coma—before Hannah Stelling could tell him she was pregnant with their child. Now she's back in town and Mark's recovered. While Hannah knows their little boy needs his father, will she dare to risk her heart again?

SNOWBOUND WITH THE BEST MAN
Matrimony Valley • by Allie Pleiter

Widower Bruce Lohan plans to use his friend's small-town wedding weekend to bond with his little girl. But when they're snowed in and his daughter befriends florist Kelly Nelson's daughter, the two little matchmakers become determined that Bruce and Kelly will be the next to wed.

A BABY FOR THE MINISTER
by Laurel Blount

Jilted at the altar, Natalie Davis has no one she can turn to. Then Jacob Stone steps in. The single minister is drawn to the beautiful mommy-to-be and wants to help. But when she refuses to accept charity, can he convince her she's so much more than a ministry project?